Cindy Lawton Mysteries

BOOK ONE

The Inheritance

by

Barbara M. Olson

DORRANCE PUBLISHING CO., INC.
PITTSBURGH, PENNSYLVANIA 15222

This is a work of fiction. Names, characters, places, and incidents are either the product of the author's imagination or are used fictitiously, and any resemblance to actual persons, living or dead; events; or locales is entirely coincidental.

Dedication

To Gloria Morrison
without whose help and support
this and the following adventures of
Cindy and Rene would not be possible.

All Rights Reserved
Copyright © 2001 by Barbara M. Olson
No part of this book may be reproduced or transmitted
in any form or by any means, electronic or mechanical,
including photocopying, recording, or by any information
storage and retrieval system without permission in
writing from the publisher.

ISBN # 0-8059-5487-5550-X
Printed in the United States of America

First Printing
For information or to order additional books, please write:
Dorrance Publishing Co., Inc.
643 Smithfield Street
Pittsburgh, Pennsylvania 15222
U.S.A.
1-800-788-7654
Or visit our web site and on-line catalog at www.dorrancepublishing.com

Main Characters

Cindy Lawton

Rene Ford

Elizabeth Hargrove

Edna – Elizabeth's maid

Mable – Elizabeth's cook

Sam – Mable's grandson

Wykoff sisters

Hinkle & Hinkle Attorneys

Lea – president of Habitat

Sicky – small-time thief

Tom Hastings – Sid's boss

Judge Harry Thompson

Benny – Attorney General

Matt – Rene's son

Dick and Nora – handyman and cook

Tim Monohan

Mayor J.P. Anthony III

Fred Blackstone – accountant

Shirley – Fred's wife

Jerry and Jan Stencil – motorcyclists

Chapter One

It had been raining since Cindy left the ship and headed home. Even Georgia with its turbulence seemed to be trying to pull her down into a depressing mood. It was one of those wet spring days that were supposed to bring May flowers, but standing next to the casket of Elizabeth, a lady who meant a great deal to Cindy, was not her idea of enjoying the rainy morning. She normally would read by a fire in her cozy little home on such a day as this.

The mourners were all known to Cindy. Some were ladies from her church, whom she had introduced five years before to Elizabeth. The little ladies, elderly, well-groomed with their white hair pinned under trim little hats, had shrunk through the ages. Elizabeth's entire staff was also in full attendance.

Standing at a respectable distance behind Cindy and the church ladies stood twelve motorcycles. The black-suited men would have appeared to be local businessmen, if you had not seen them arrive on their noisy motorcycles, which were all black or draped in a black material. Black armbands were on their sleeves. Eight had carried the casket while the remaining four had led the procession to the gravesite. Those four were the ones to lower Elizabeth into her grave. It was obvious these men were taking her death with difficulty by the many tears flowing unheeded down their faces. Cindy had known about the motorcycle gang, but had never seen them in this large a number.

Cindy stood taller than most of the mourners in her two-inch-heeled boots. She usually stood out in a group, being six-feet in her stockinged feet. She wore an all black pantsuit. Her attire had changed very little over the years. She didn't own a dress and found no reason to purchase one for today, knowing she would never wear it again. After her long flight she had made an attempt to smooth the wrinkles from her jacket and pants before getting out of the car, but it was a fruitless effort as the more it rained the more disheveled she looked.

Her best friend Rene Ford told her she should get some color in her wardrobe, and Cindy's comment was, "It might detract from my mystique." Her friend had laughed at her and gave up trying to improve her.

Cindy's copper-red hair, cut short in stylish tiers, stuck to her head as the rain kept pouring. She never carried an umbrella for she always lost them. Today she wished she had. She thought she was not an emotional person, but the tears on her cheeks blended with the raindrops into a continuous river, cascading down her face. She could not stop crying regardless how hard she tried.

It was another horrible death she had to face in less than a dozen years. First there was the husband of her best friend, Rene. He had died after a long illness that had sapped the life from him and left him a shell of a man. Then came her husband Herb's mysterious death, and now Elizabeth. Being an only child, who lost her parents before her thirteenth birthday, she found that death came a little harder for her each time.

Cindy, a real estate appraiser, met Elizabeth five years before when Elizabeth called to have her large, Victorian house and estate appraised. She soon realized, after being with her only a short time, that Elizabeth needed company far more than an appraisal of her property. Elizabeth was tiny-framed, with thick, pure white hair, sparkling deep blue eyes, and dimpled cheeks. She always wore a smile on her lips and quiet, gray, tailored suits on her body. The only color she used with her wardrobe was an occasional small pink silk scarf around her throat. The first time Cindy met Elizabeth she fell in love with her immediately. She soon counted her as one of her closest friends, even though there was a forty-five year span between their ages.

Cindy adored the house almost as much as she adored Elizabeth and visited as often as possible. She recalled the first time she saw the house and met the lovely lady. It was on a Monday. Cindy received Elizabeth's call on the previous Wednesday, but had a very full calendar and couldn't get to the estate any sooner due to a backlog of appointments.

She arrived at the mansion at about 10:00 in the morning and parked her car on the side under the overhanging roof. She had to set her emergency brake when she realized the slope of the old brick drive caused her car to roll backward out from under the portico. Since this was to be an appraisal, Cindy took note of the deteriorating driveway. She observed everything around her with a professional eye. She walked up a front carriage porch that covered a third of the house. Knocking at the towering, twelve-foot, solid oak doors, she waited. A maid answered, opening only one of the doors barely enough to allow Cindy to enter. She walked into the entrance hall/reception area. It looked to be at least forty feet long and approximately thirty feet deep. A large, seven-tiered crystal chandelier hung at the foot of the stairs. It was a work of art, multi-branched in a Baroque style; in silver, gold, and rock crystal, with porcelain and crystal prisms. It was almost eight feet wide and stood well over four feet high. The chandelier had been converted to electricity and updated somewhere around the 1800s. Its small twin hung half way up the first flight of stairs, with an even smaller version hanging at the top of the risers. The house was a treasure of chandeliers.

The marble floors and skip-plastered walls gave the room a very warm appearance especially in an entrée room of this size. Cindy remembered watching a skip plasterer apply similar walls several months earlier, and commented to him how becoming they looked. He told her the only way to do a good job was to put the plaster on, then do a lousy job with the trowel. Regardless it enhanced the charm of the foyer. Although Cindy would have preferred all wood walls and ceilings, and she wondered why they had elected to plaster the room when wood was noticeably present everywhere else. She was an avid woodworker and would put everything in wood if it were her choice.

At the top of the stairs, stained glass windows spewed a shower of color over the first floor landing and down the stairway. The view was awesome which must have been the effect the builder had in mind when he designed it originally. The wide, English staircase was centered in the middle of the room and set back from the front doors about fifteen feet. It was of a warm oak wood with a twelve-foot runner of plush, tea rose-patterned, Axminister weave carpet, in burgundy-pink that ran down the middle with a three-foot strip of oak flooring showing down each side. Everything looked a little tattered and worn, but Cindy knew it had, at one time, been the town showplace.

The windows were enhanced by sheers hanging beneath heavy brocade drapes. *I would have put antique sateen on the rods,* she thought, *but then I guess the room might look too modern. No, it should remain as is. The effect is definitely seventeenth century and goes with the old castle façade.*

The oak staircase, with its twisted rails, had been rubbed through the years to a seasoned hue, glowing from constant care. The floor was white marble with a gray vein running throughout it. Two other rooms were found in the same warm oak. The room at the end of the entrée was used as a parlor with a side music room. The ceilings were of carved rosette pattern in ten-inch squares with an eighteen-inch crown molding around the top of the wall. The same hue appeared on the ceiling. She again noted the many years of hand-rubbing the surface with oils. The other wood room was the library. It served as an office for the master of the house when he was alive. It was located at the opposite end of the long reception area. It had wall-to-ceiling bookshelves on the north wall, with a tower stairway in the corner. The small stairway lead to a little retreat at the top of the turret, with a view of the west garden. A sixteenth century traveling desk was in one corner, with a small, platform rocker used as a desk chair. He had the walls done in Cyprus and the room had an enchanting air about it. A mauve, royal blue, and kelly green Oriental rug accented the furniture groupings, making the room exude a feeling of welcome. She could have spent hours in that special room, it was so inviting and restful.

Cindy felt like it was all a dream. It was actually a small castle more than forty thousand-eight hundred square feet and four stories high, set in the deep woods of the exclusive Wykoff Estates, within twenty miles of a going north vacation spot.

Chapter Two

Edna, Elizabeth's personal maid, was enjoying her holiday at the Wykoff Park with her sister and her sister's grandchildren when she saw the police car drive into Wykoff Estates.

Old Mr. Wykoff, many years before he died, had designated five acres on each side of the estates' main entrance for a community park. It had a little stream on one side of the road for the children to fish. The townspeople saw to it that the stream always had fish for the little ones to catch. They put up swings, slides, teeter-totters, and picnic tables. The park, on the other side of the road, had three baseball diamonds for the little league. It was the site to which everyone from town came on weekends. They took great pride in keeping the grounds cared for and frowned at any outsiders who did not do likewise.

Edna had packed Mrs. Elizabeth for the trip she was to take on Thursday. Since her mistress had no further need of her services for the rest of the week, she was excused on Friday. Edna only worked five days a week and always spent the weekend with her sister and family. She had never been married or had children of her own, so she enjoyed spoiling her grandnieces and nephew. Her sister told her continually that she should save her money, but on what else was she going to spend it? They were the only real family she had. Her parents were long gone.

Edna saw two more police cars drive in, followed by the coroner's car.

She told her sister, "It must be the Wykoff sisters. I'd better go see if I can help. No matter which sister is ill, the other sister is going to need someone. They are so close and her maid is quite elderly. I'll be back shortly."

After helping round up the children and seeing that they were back with their grandmother, she borrowed her sister's car and went back into Wykoff estates. The police cars were not in the Wykoff sisters' drive, so she continued to her employer's home and found them in Elizabeth's drive.

What in the world could have happened? she wondered.

The other estate across the road was closed. The owners went on vacations at this time of year. Edna thought that maybe a vagrant had slipped into one of the back gates.

She drove up the drive and stopped behind the coroner's car. "What's going on here?" she asked.

"The old lady's been killed. Who are you?" a young police officer bluntly asked.

"That's Edna—Mrs. Elizabeth's personal maid," the coroner said. "What brings you back today, Edna?"

"I was in the park and saw all the police cars. I thought one of the Wykoff sisters had taken ill. I came to see if the other sister needed my help, and when I saw you parked at Mrs. Elizabeth's, I came here. What is going on? May I be of service?" she asked again.

"Only if you can tell us who killed her," the young policeman said.

"Who killed who?"

"Someone killed Mrs. Hargrove," the coroner told her.

"That is crazy, everyone loved my mistress," Edna grabbed her heart. "Are you sure?"

It was too much for her.

"Yes? I'm afraid it is, Edna," the coroner said. "I'm sorry."

He put his arm around the maid's shoulders.

"Vagrants come about this time of year to help prepare the land we farm. They always make me nervous, but they are a necessity. Maybe it is one of those motorcycle people. I can't understand why Mrs. Elizabeth was home. She was to have been on a cruise; that's why the whole staff was gone. We were given our vacation and I was allowed to leave early."

She could not believe all that was happening and was babbling.

"I knew she was too good to people; always having anyone in for tea."

"What motorcycle people?" the officer asked.

"The local gang." The coroner smiled. He knew the so-called gang, and admired all they did for the community's young people.

"I can't, really I can't," she cried as the realization of what happened began to seep into her consciousness.

"That won't be necessary," the coroner said. "If you'd been here longer, you'd know that it is Mrs. Elizabeth," he scowled to the young officer.

He put his arm through Edna's, helping her into the house and over to the parlor, where he deposited her in a chair.

"Who all knew Mrs. Elizabeth didn't take the cruise?" he asked her.

"No one I can think of, except maybe Mrs. Lawton. They were to take the cruise together. You might call her; maybe the cruise was canceled," Edna suggested.

"Mrs. Lawton is on the cruise," he told her. "She is why we stopped out. She called the precinct when she couldn't get Mrs. Elizabeth on a ship-to-shore phone."

"Hold it, let's not tell everything we know," the young lieutenant said. "Remember everyone is a suspect." He turned to Edna. "Call anyone you can get a hold of and get them back here," he demanded, "pronto!"

"You might ask her a little nicer," the old coroner said. "This is a small community up here, and her employees have worked for Mrs. Elizabeth for twenty years or more; they will be anxious to cooperate." He turned to Edna. "Do you think many stayed in town?"

"I don't think so, sir. I know most went down to the condo's in Florida for three weeks. Mrs. Elizabeth owns a group of condos outside Crystal River, Florida, and allows us to spend our vacations there each year; I was to join them next week. I saw the taxis take some of them to the airport myself while I was shopping in town on Saturday. They waved to me as they passed. We were all so happy Mrs. Elizabeth had found a young traveling companion. I have no idea what happened or why she didn't leave with Mrs. Lawton."

"So you said," the officer stared at her. "I'll need you to follow us downtown and start calling around."

"That won't be necessary, sir. Mrs. Elizabeth has a direct line to the condos," she told him. "All you need do is push #10 on auto dial and it rings through to the management office."

"Well try to round up as many as you can find. Maybe someone can tell us something. We'll keep Lawton on ice for today. She can't go anywhere. The ship won't be in a port for two more days. Tomorrow is soon enough. It will give us a little head-start, if she is involved," the officer said.

Edna gave the officer an inquiring look and said, "I feel obligated to tell you, sir, that Mrs. Lawton was wonderful to our mistress and got her back into a social life. She took her places and spent many evenings here, eating, talking, and playing games. Mrs. Elizabeth loved her and enjoyed every minute Mrs. Lawton spent with her. That is why it is so strange Mrs. Elizabeth was not with Mrs. Lawton."

"Yeah! Real strange," he stated critically. "Get a hold of the staff, now! What are you waiting for?"

Edna did not like this young man's attitude. She was not used to being addressed so rudely. Mrs. Elizabeth never failed to say "please" and "thank you" when making a request to one of the servants.

Breeding shows, she thought and went over to the phone. She punched #10 and found out that all the old staff were staying at the condos. She told them what she knew, hung up the phone, and turned to the coroner.

"They will be flying back together tomorrow, and will be at the manor by noon."

The coroner suggested the police do the staff interrogations at the manor.

The next afternoon they interviewed each one but couldn't find one who could have flown back and killed the woman.

"They all alibi one another," the frustrated officer said. "Their units were next door to one another and they either fished or joined each other for meals every day. It would be impossible for any one of them to fly back and forth in less than eight hours. I checked with the field and found no one fitting any of their descriptions who had flown in on the midnight run."

It was a small airport and the attendants could identify anyone who may have flown in on a plane day or night.

"It looks like Mrs. Lawton is our best bet. She must have had an accomplice," the lieutenant said.

The officers went to Mrs. Hawthorn's attorney's office next. After spending twenty minutes with the old attorney, they returned to their car.

The lieutenant looked at the coroner and said, "See! I was right."

Chapter Three

Elizabeth's death was a shock to her neighbors and friends in the small town. She had been robbed and beaten, even after she had died. The thieves evidently did not know they had killed her with the first blow. She had fallen in the front foyer and hit her head on the marble floor.

Cindy made up her mind someone was going to pay for killing that sweet old lady. She would have to do the investigating herself, since she didn't have much faith that the local police department could track an elephant after a snow storm.

The ladies were beginning to leave and the servants were scowling at Cindy as they walked by her. She couldn't understand their attitude. They had to know how dear Elizabeth had been to her.

The staff was going to the mansion for coffee and the reading of the will. Cindy had asked to be excused, but the family retainers insisted she attend. They also asked Jerry Stencil, leader of the local motorcycle gang, to be present. Cindy had driven her old black LTD classic to the funeral, so she would drive herself to the estate. The car was the first gift Herb received from her. She had been appraising an old farm and found it parked out in the side pasture. She took it in place of her fee. For more than a year her own car sat out in the weather, while she and Herb restored the old Ford. It was his pride and joy. After his untimely death, the death the local police called an "accident," she went everywhere in the LTD. It made her feel closer to Herb and was a constant reminder of her love for him. She was sure he had been murdered. The coroner could not, or would not, determine the cause of death. Herb had hit a guardrail which prevented his car from rolling down the embankment. If it had gone over the steep hill, it very likely would have destroyed the car. In truth there was very little damage to Herb or to the body of the car.

He had been on a deserted dirt road, out in the country, around two in the morning. The coroner called it accidental death; everything had just shut down and he died before anyone found him. The police found it easy to say he fell asleep at the wheel, but Cindy knew they were wrong. Herb had worked midnights for more than a year and was used to the long night hours. They found no drugs or alcohol in his body. She knew they wouldn't, as neither he nor Cindy thought they were necessary substances and avoided most anyone who did indulge. She had loved him madly and missed him terribly. Someday she would find out the truth about his death, since it was evident to her that the police were hiding something. He was a good detective and had probably been working on a case when he was killed. Until she knew the truth, she could not lay him to rest in her mind. She had to find out what he was involved in, what would lead him out there at such an hour.

As she started to pull away from the funeral, Jerry knocked on her passenger side window. Cindy rolled down the window.

"May I ride with you?" he asked. "The rain is really pouring now, and I'll be a wet mop by the time I get there."

"Of course," Cindy said.

She knew he carried a slicker on his bike and could have worn it, but she wanted to hear what he had on his mind. She closed the window and leaned over and unlocked the passenger door.

Jerry sat down on the bench seat and put on his seat belt.

"Thank you," he said "I didn't want to ask any of the staff. They are all scared to death of us. Whenever we visited Mrs. Elizabeth, they would all disappear until we left. Edna was the only one brave enough to serve us tea and cookies."

Cindy smiled to herself. She could just imagine those big, beefy, leather-clad men drinking tea and eating cookies in the Elizabeth's dainty parlor. She wondered how they could get their big fingers to hold the tiny cups and saucers without breaking them. It must have been some sight.

Jerry was the first to change the conversation from small talk to the death of Elizabeth.

"Who do you think did it, Mrs. Lawton?" he asked.

"Cindy! Please call me Cindy," she told him. "I honestly don't know, Jerry. She was so well loved. It must have been an outsider."

Jerry's eyes misted over.

"She was so good to our organization. She never once looked down on us."

"Why would she. You don't cause any trouble and you do great work with the youth in the community. There is only one difference between your gang and the rest of us; you always wear leather and ride big cycles," Cindy said. "I am curious about one thing though, Jerry, if you don't mind me asking."

"How did we meet Mrs. Elizabeth?"

Cindy smiled, "Yes! A lot of us have wondered about that."

"It's kind of a boring story, but I don't mind telling you. I was riding downtown with about six of the gang, when she walked out in front of my bike. I had to swerve and lay it down to keep from hitting her. When I laid it on its side, two other bikes ran it over. We were all three lying in the road when she walked up to me and gave me her hand to help me. I almost laughed. If I had taken her hand, I would have pulled her on top of me, she was so tiny."

Cindy smiled at the thought. "Then what happened?"

"She insisted she wanted to fix all three bikes, and invited us out to the manor. She said she had two old bikes and a sidecar in her back garage and demanded we take them until ours were fixed. When we got out there one of her servants escorted us to the barn and showed us two old Pan Harleys, complete with an old sidecar. They had to be more than thirty years old, but after a little work, they kicked right over and we drove them to the side door of the house. She asked us in for tea. We were a little hesitant; not about the tea, but none of us had been in a place like that."

"I can well imagine," Cindy said. "I see a lot of fine homes in my business, but I was a little awestruck when I first saw it, too. I'm sorry, I didn't mean to interrupt. Please continue."

"There is not much more to tell. She would not let us give the bikes back to her. She said she was so glad someone was using them. She couldn't ride any more and lost interest in them when her husband died. I guess it was something they had enjoyed doing together. She would have us out several times a year for lunch, and twice a year she gave us a check for our kid's charity. She said she didn't want us driving out there at night since it was too dark. Can you believe that? She worried about us riding our bikes at night," he smiled.

"Yes! That sounds like her. I have one more question. Did you give her a leather motorcycle jacket?"

"Yes and no. We wanted to give her one that fit her, but she said she wanted it larger. We gave her one and, when she tried it on, she said it was perfect and thanked us. It was at least five sizes too big for her. We never could figure out why she wanted it so large."

"I can," Cindy said. "She gave it to me."

"You're kidding?" Jerry smiled. "I guess now you will have to buy a bike to go with it."

"Ha! I can barely afford my house payments. I don't need the luxury of a bike."

"Well, when you're ready, I can return today's favor and give you a ride on mine," he said. "That way you can use your jacket."

They rode the remainder of the trip in relative silence, both thinking about their old friend.

Chapter Four

Arriving back at the house, Cindy found that the staff and attorneys were there, seated in the library. She stood just inside the double doors and leaned back against the dark mahogany wall. She felt its coolness against her nylon blouse. She had placed her jacket in the back seat before entering. Jerry stood leaning against the wall on the other side of the door.

The eldest Hinkle of Hinkle and Sons Attorneys at Law spotted her and told someone to move and Cindy to take the vacated chair up front, since she might need to be seated where she could hear everything. It was going to take a while to read the will. Cindy did as she was told. She sat down, crossed her long legs, and tried to look alert. Wills and exercise were in the same category for her; both boring. She found no reason she should have to endure the reading. All she wanted to do was go home, sit in her easy chair, put her feet up, and have a good cry.

After much fanfare and deep explanations about Elizabeth's lack of relatives and her being of sound mind and body, he started to read the will.

He should be as sound, Cindy thought.

Mr. Hinkle came to the part where Elizabeth designated $50,000 to the little Baptist church on the hill, where she and Cindy were regular members. Another $50,000 was to be given to the local motorcycle club, hence Jerry's reason for being invited. Jerry looked like he was in a state of shock. Cindy knew that he and his friends received $4,000 twice a year from Elizabeth for their young people's group, but $50,000?

If they invested it wisely, they could go on indefinitely; that must have been Elizabeth's idea, Cindy thought.

Jerry was so pleased, he stood there grinning through the remainder of the reading.

The servants had been with Elizabeth since her marriage to Jasper fifty odd years before and, after his death seven years previous, they became part of her family. In part two of the will, she left them all one million dollars, tax free; along with a condo for each, at a complex she owned in Crystal River, Florida. A gasp came out of several of the servants' mouths, joined by Jerry and Cindy.

Talk about a sweet retirement package, Cindy's mind mused; but she was happy for them since she knew how devoted they had been to Elizabeth.

"There was only one stipulation in the will," the attorney stated. "The present staff has to stay until the new owner can acquire a staff."

In part three, Mr. Hinkle went on to explain the remainder of the estate and all holdings were to be left to Elizabeth's best friend, Cindy Lawton.

"Who?" Cindy yelled.

Her legs uncrossed and, jumping to her feet, she started arguing with the attorneys. "There has to be some mistake. I couldn't possibly accept all this. Even if I wanted to, I would never be able to keep this place up. It will need almost a million dollars to renovate it back to its original condition. I told Elizabeth as much on my first visit. There must be some living relatives somewhere!"

The lawyer only smiled at her and said "There aren't, and the will is air tight. When Elizabeth's accounting firm contacts you, they will assure you the interest alone on Elizabeth's holdings will more than pay for any remodeling, and still cover all costs of running such an estate for the next two hundred years."

Cindy was to find out later that Elizabeth held property and rentals in thirty states; and had invested in very lucrative stocks, bonds, and numerous CDs. She was beginning to understand why the servants were so cool toward her, and why the police had taken such an active interest in her recent whereabouts. They were not looking too hard for Elizabeth's killer, they figured they had one. Much smaller fortunes than this one had been excuses for murder. She really had her work cut out for her. She didn't need all this hassle right now. Hadn't she had enough for one morning, with Elizabeth's death and now this? Not only did she have a heavy caseload, but she was going to have to find Elizabeth's killer before the police lowered the boom on her. She now knew why they insisted she give them her itinerary for the last week, along with the motels and planes she had used on her vacation. She had thought they were just interested, since she was to have taken Elizabeth with her.

Due to a nasty cold Elizabeth had contacted, she had decided to stay home for the first week of the cruise and was to join Cindy for the last two weeks. When Elizabeth had to postpone her trip, she insisted Cindy go on without her. Cindy knew most of the servants were to take their vacation before Elizabeth left, leaving her alone on the estate; but Cindy was assured that either Edna or Mary would stay until Elizabeth flew out to join her.

Cindy hated to fly alone in the big commercial planes, so she rented a car and drove down to Florida. She thought of renting a plane, since she had a small craft license, but decided it would be cheaper to drive; and take time to see some of the sights on the way. She stayed the second night in Cleveland, Tennessee, and toured one of the gem mines. Leaving the next day and driving the remainder of the way straight through, she turned in the rental car that evening and went immediately to the ship.

Cindy tried to reach her by the ship-to-shore phone for two days and finally called the local police, asking them to go to the house and check on Elizabeth. She was savoring a wonderful lobster bisque when the steward called her away from the captain's table and notified her of Elizabeth's death. She hired a helicopter to take her to the nearest airport. Two days later she was standing at the grave.

When the attorney finished, Cindy walked in a daze to her car with a hundred thoughts going through her head. *Whatever was Elizabeth thinking, leaving her estate to me? I have never kept more than a three-bedroom house in my entire life, and I still owe payments on it. Where should I begin? What should I do? I know, she figured I'd renovate the old place to its original splendor. We often talked about what she would like to do if she was younger. Well, I'm younger but I know beans about property, taxes, and rentals. I'm going to be hopping around like a bag of jumping beans. I better call Rene and get her up here, stat. Rene knows accounting at least.*

"Boy! I can't even imagine how I would handle all the book work required in running an estate of this magnitude," she said out loud to herself, "and I don't think I want to know."

As she and Jerry walked out to her car, he smiled and said, "Now you can afford a cycle."

Cindy didn't answer. She drove him back to the cemetery and later could not remember any of their conversation from the return trip. After dropping him off, she turned on her car radio, trying to relax her active brain. The radio was on a rock station and it came blaring out at her.

"Ouch," she said as she turned the dial to her favorite station.

Chapter Five

Arriving back at her home around 5:00 P.M., Cindy kicked off her boots, threw her black pantsuit on the bed, and climbed into her black sweat pants and matching pullover. One nice thing about owning only black, white, and gray clothes, she never had to worry if her outfits matched properly. The other nine pair of boots in her closet were also combinations of gray, white, and black. If she ever wore a different color, no one would recognize her. Except for her height, red hair, and deep-set dimples, she was pretty ordinary looking. While holding a modeling job a few years back, she had been told that her brown eyes were her best feature, and the agents thought she was quite attractive with makeup; but it took too much time, so she seldom was "all made up." Tossing cold water on her face, she toweled the dampness back into her hair. The red glistened in the mirror.

She went into the kitchen and found that she neither had the ambition nor the appetite for cooking a meal. She rummaged through the partially empty cupboards. She was really low on supplies and made a mental note to stop at the grocery first thing in the morning. She had not expected to be home for a month or more. Finally finding a bag of microwave popcorn, she nuked it while boiling water for decaf tea. She found the tea, frozen, in the top of her refrigerator. She always put it in the freezer when she was going to be gone for a few days. She had her dinner ready in six minutes.

Cindy carried her meal into the living room. Taking her remote fire starter to her favorite chair, she turned on the gas fireplace and sat in the old recliner. It had been Herb's chair and she refused to recover it since it still smelled of his shampoo. She reached down and lifted the footrest, leaned back, and picked up the book she had bought onboard ship. Her eye caught the flicker of her answering machine. Its pulsating beat seemed to call out to her.

With a deep sigh she pushed the blinking button. She must have quite a few calls since it took several seconds to rewind before the first voice sounded. She recognized the name, but not the voice. She only met Elizabeth's neighbors, the Wykoff sisters, once. Now they were her new next-door neighbors. She smiled to herself since she had not realized until just now that she had decided to move into the old manor. The message on the answering machine stated that the sisters needed to see her right away and would she please call A.S.A.P. They had probably heard about her inheritance and wanted to know all the details. She'd call them in the morning. She was in no mood for conversation tonight.

The next call was from the Bradfords, across the street from her new estate. She had not realized they were back from their vacation. They must have seen all the excitement at Elizabeth's. News sure travels fast in Wykoff estates; she would have to remember that. Any disturbances caused nervous frustration with the residents. The last call was from Elizabeth's accountant and financial adviser, wanting an appointment, also A.S.A.P. They could all wait till morning; she was just going to flop the rest of the evening; that thought wasn't even a memory when the phone rang. It was the Wykoffs again.

Sylvia said, "Would you come over immediately? We need an appraisal on our estate, and we don't want to wait another day."

Cindy wondered why the sisters were in such a hurry.

"It will take me at least two days to get all the papers and comparables on your property," she told them.

They didn't care; they wanted her over there now. She finally gave in and told them she could be there in about an hour. Back into the bedroom she went, slipping off her comfies and taking up the black jumpsuit she had worn to the funeral. She exchanged the bolero jacket she normally wore with it for her black suede blazer with the gray, patched sleeves; and selected her black and gray boots. Her purse was black so she looked very nice, not too chic, but not sporty either; almost like a business woman. She smiled at her reflection in the mirror.

Climbing into her LTD, she smelled that scant odor of cigarette smoke again. It was the second time today she had smelled stale smoke in her car. Jerry had asked her if she smoked. He must have smelled it also. She rolled the windows down and tried to blow the stench out. When had she been where a valet could have driven her car and smoked a cigarette? She remembered she had cleaned it, inside and out, just before her trip and had it stored in the garage during her absence. It gave her an eerie feeling, as if someone also had been in her house while she was gone.

She thought she could smell the odor in the house, too; when she first arrived back from the funeral. The security system was working when she opened the door after returning from the funeral. It must just be her imagination working over time again. It had the habit of doing that often since Herb's death. She had hoped the feelings would go away, since they were making her a very jumpy lady. She believed she was also being watched since her return; and she probably was, she decided.

"The police don't have anything better to do with their time," she said out loud as she watched a car pull from the curb and fall in two cars behind her.

She was going to have to stop talking to herself out loud or people would begin to worry about her, but as Rene always told her, "You get better answers that way."

A smile crossed her face for the second time today as she thought of her old friend, Rene Ford.

She called her Rene because her son had a hard time saying her full name when he first started talking and the tag had stuck. Cindy was over at Rene's every day for the first couple weeks after Matt's birth. She fed him, diapered him, and let him nap lying on her chest. The bond between them was so strong they called one another every week to be sure the other was okay. Rene didn't seem to mind and was pleased that Cindy enjoyed her son. Cindy bought him his first two-wheeler and Rene feared that a five-year-old was too young. Matt hopped on it and rode off. When he took his driver's test, he took Cindy's car. When he bought his own car, he called her for advice. When he went to the prom, he asked her to pick out his tux. After Matt's father's death, Rene was happy he had someone besides herself to talk to and knew Cindy would always check with her before giving any serious advice or gifts to her son. The two women loved each other dearly and Cindy was thankful Rene was willing to share Matt.

Chapter Six

Cindy drove up the drive at Wykoff's. She didn't put on the emergency brake as she did at Elizabeth's; there was no need. The Wykoffs had a nice new asphalt drive, and it didn't have that strange slope of Elizabeth's old brick and sand driveway.

Cindy was greeted at the front door by a maid in a starched white and black uniform, complete with a tiny matching bonnet. Standing on the old carriage porch, she felt she had stepped back in time. There was not the warm feeling in the entry hall like there was at Elizabeth's. The maid, who should have retired years ago, had a superior, cold attitude toward Cindy. Any warmth from her for another human had long since left her.

When Cindy entered, both sisters came walking down the arched, circular stairway, one on the left side and one on the right. They both wore skirts that swept the ground, with matching high-collared blouses and smart patent leather slippers. One sister wore blue and the other yellow. Except for the color of their outfits; they were identical. She wondered if they each had separate apartments in the wings, on either side of the stairs. Sylvia was the first to speak, which was not unusual, Cindy discovered. Blanch was much quieter and always left Sylvia to take the lead. Cindy favored Blanch at their only previous meeting. Sylvia was a little too overpowering.

They both greeted her warmly and escorted her to the sitting-room at the right of the large hall. It was heavy with brocade-upholstered chairs and a matching love seat. There was not a warm feeling in any of the furnishings either.

They chatted about the weather until tea was served. The room was well-used and faced Elizabeth's house. There was a large, high-powered telescope in the window facing Elizabeth's manor.

Everyone in town knew the sisters spent their spare hours checking out the neighborhoods and the park. It was their harmless pastime and everyone overlooked it. It was like having their own "Neighborhood Watch." During the summer months you would not have been able to see the manor, but without the foliage on the trees, the telescope gave a very clear view of part of Cindy's property and a small section of the house.

After tea, Sylvia came to the real reason for their phone call. They wanted to get out of the area where a murder had taken place.

"Who knows what kind of people will be our new next door neighbors?" she said. "It could be some rowdy dope dealers. They are the only ones who seem to have that kind of money anymore."

Cindy smiled pleasantly and told them she wasn't rowdy or a dope pusher. "I don't smoke or drink."

Both sisters started talking and asking questions at once.

"Please let me explain," she said. "I did not realize Elizabeth felt so deeply about me, but she did and she left her entire estate in my hands. I plan on doing my very best to restore it to its original splendor. I will be moving in as soon as possible."

Being very outspoken, Sylvia said, "How in the world will you ever do that, are you going to quit your job? You know it will be a full-time job just to run that place. I know of over one hundred-ten acres, with orchards, gardens, and an airstrip; plus the several farms Elizabeth owned right here in Wykoff Acres. Heaven only knows what else she owns. She and Mr. Hargrove were always very business-minded. Taking trips to other states and even after he was gone, she traveled with her attorneys."

Cindy had not considered she might have to quit her job. She enjoyed her work and would miss it. She informed them as much; and as for having the time, she planned on bringing a whole new staff in to help.

"The present staff will be retiring to Florida," she told them.

She sat back and let them digest all the gossip. She sipped the tea the maid had just poured and picked up a small cookie from the silver tray. Their maid Alice looked even older than the sisters and had never been employed anywhere else.

Elizabeth had told her once that Alice had been the ladies' playmate when they were children. She was the daughter of the sister's governess. As they grew older, and the governess died, the sisters asked Alice to stay on as a "lady in waiting." Alice had nowhere else to go. She had never lived anywhere but at Wykoff Manor. She was thankful the sisters had figured a way to keep her near them. They were all three very set in their ways and it was obvious they did not know quite how to react to this latest change.

The sisters' grandfather had built and named the entire development; he even named two of the streets after his granddaughters. It must have been a disappointment when the large acreage he worked so hard to develop did not grow like he expected. Few wealthy businessmen from down below wanted the remote area. He often thought it was their pampered, society-minded wives who refused to come this far north for a retreat. Their wives' idea of a leisurely vacation was on a yacht or in the south of France. "Who wants another residence to look after, and as far as retiring in 'boonsville,' you can forget it," as more than one wife so delicately put it.

Cindy smiled at the three and said, "You must remember, ladies, you've known your staff for years and are comfortable with them. It would be a crime to move from this lovely home. You have resided at Wykoff all of your lives. You will never be happy anywhere else."

No one ever left Wykoff Estates, except in a pine box, but that she didn't mention.

"I would hate not having you beautiful ladies next door. I am probably being selfish, but there is so much I can learn from the three of you. I was hoping I could depend on you if I have difficulties adjusting; and I will, in turn, always be available if you should need me," Cindy told them. "If I might make a suggestion?" she added. "You may want to invest in a security system, if it would make you feel more secure. You could also get a chauffeur again, so there would be a man on the premises. It's a shame not to use that beautiful Cadillac limo Elizabeth told me you owned. If for no other reason but getting out in the fresh air. If you're not using one of the guest houses I observed as I drove onto the estate, you might even find a married couple to live in it."

She continued, "He could drive you wherever you needed to go and his wife could relieve Alice by running errands for you ladies. They could be a real asset. Most men can fix little things around the house and grounds that you have to hire outsiders to attend to."

They pondered the information for several minutes. Both sisters perked up and it was clear Alice thought it to be a great idea, showing the first emotion Cindy had seen since she arrived.

Just as Cindy was about to leave, Blanch said, "I told Sylvia you were the person to talk to," she said. "You seemed so nice the time we met you in the yard. After all, you were kind enough to loan your beautiful LTD to Mable's grandson Sam while you went on vacation."

Mable was Elizabeth's cook and Sam was a trouble-making juvenile and also the last person to whom Cindy would loan a classic automobile.

"When did you see Sam in my car, dear?" Cindy asked, trying not to let her voice waver. The sisters could not have guessed how important the question was to Cindy.

"Why he drove into Elizabeth's driveway the day after you left. I wouldn't have noticed, but he swore when the car started to roll backward down the drive. His companion yelled, 'Put on the emergency brake, stupid.' We heard him because we have the scanner on our new telescope a little too high. We sometimes like to listen to the trees. Their music makes a lovely background while we read."

Cindy almost laughed and reminded herself never to say anything she didn't want overheard; at least while in the driveway of her new house.

She thanked them for the tea, trying to leave as quickly as possible. She asked them to think about the security measures and to consider staying her neighbor.

"I can help look for a couple if you wish. I'll also get in touch with the same security company I will be using."

They both answered together, "Oh! We are staying."

"If you would call for us, it would be very kind of you," said Sylvia. "We have never had any dealing with security companies and we would not know where to begin. With the way things are today, it is probably imperative we take appropriate measures."

Cindy excused herself and left three much happier ladies than those whom she met when she arrived. They were not the only ones who were happier; Cindy now knew her imagination was not running wild. She left the house; got into her car; and headed directly to police headquarters.

On the way to town Cindy called the Bradfords on her car phone and explained all that she knew, omitting the clue the Wykoffs had just revealed to her.

Mr. Bradford informed her, "We saw your car at Elizabeth's the day after you were supposed to have left, but it looked like two young men were in it. We were pulling out of our drive when the men blew the horn and whizzed by us."

Now she was in a bigger hurry to get to the police station. She rang off, promising she would get back to them soon since she was on her way to town on an important errand. She thanked him for his interest and pushed the end button on her cell phone.

He turned to his wife and said, "She is our new neighbor."

"Who dear?" she asked.

"The redhead," he smiled and informed her of Elizabeth's will.

Chapter Seven

Arriving at the station, Cindy parked in the officers' lot and picked up her cell phone again. This time she called police headquarters and asked for Detective Monohan. He picked up on the first ring. He did not sound like he was in a very good humor.

"Hi, guy, how's everything?" she said cheerfully. "I hear you've been wondering about me and checking on my whereabouts."

He roared into the phone, "Where in blue blazes are you, Cindy, and what have you been up to? We've been trying to track you down for two hours; you slipped our tail. It doesn't look too good for you to be sneaking away."

"Solving your case for you," she stated.

He sure knew how to put a damper on the first good mood she had had in days. She went on to explain her visit with the sisters and her conversation with Mr. Bradford.

"Get that car in here right away and we'll dust it for prints," he said.

She laughed and told him were she was parked. Within five minutes he had the entire crew from forensics rushing out to the lot and going over her car. When they found everything had been wiped clean except for her prints, she mentioned smelling cigarette smoke in the car and at her home. They checked the ashtray; it was clean, but the lighter had a beautiful clear print that was not hers. They took her keys and got another partial off of them. It seemed one print was probably of a southpaw and showed on the back of her silver-framed key-ring case. Cindy was right-handed. The police had come up with the idea of the key ring or maybe Monohan had some investigative sense, she thought. She was willing to give him the benefit of the doubt. Cindy began to have hope for the local police force.

"Next we need to go to your house and check for prints. If there was someone smoking in your car, they probably were smoking in your house," Monohan said.

Cindy led the police back to her place. They looked like a parade of real estate salespeople on an inspection tour as they wound through the tree-lined streets. The buds were starting to appear on the trees and soon there would be a green tunnel leading to her little house. That was one of the reasons she and Herb had loved their street; in the spring it was like a welcome mat. In the fall the leaves turned gold and the sun shining down on them gave a warm, safe feeling. The tulips and jonquils were already peaking up through the soil.

Upon reaching her home, she saw many blooms she and Herb had planted starting to appear. She recognized a couple neighbors watching the entourage and she quickly explained that she was thinking of selling the house and these men were here to preview it. She wasn't lying; she might as well sell the house. She was not going to need two places to keep up, and she didn't want to live there knowing someone had been snooping into everything. It didn't seem like home anymore. She had really loved her little house and now someone had spoiled it. She'd pay it off and then talk to the local Habitat for Humanity and see if they would like it. It would be a perfect starter home for one of their applicants.

One of the neighbors walked over and said they thought she had loaned out her home while she was on the cruise. They had seen men going in and out. Two detectives asked the neighbors to describe the people using Cindy's house. They were able to give the detectives a good description of the two young men. One was fair and slightly shorter than the black-haired one. Neither seemed very well dressed, wearing filthy, torn jeans that looked like they had not been washed in weeks. The two men looked as though they had not bathed for months. The men did not appear to be the type of people with whom Cindy normally associated. The neighbors were a little upset with her. One of the neighbors said her husband started locking their doors whenever they left the house.

Cindy could well understand their apprehensions. She tried to explain she had not loaned out her home to anyone and would find out who had been trespassing.

"I told Teddy we should have reported our suspicions to the police, but he said you were always trying to help some down and out character."

Cindy smiled and gave her neighbor a hug, "Don't fret about it. I'll take care of notifying the proper authorities."

She did not tell them she had already talked to the police.

The police got lucky at the house and found several good prints. They would run them through their files as soon as they got back to the station. Cindy told them Mable's grandson might match up with one set of the prints. All but Cindy left for headquarters. She packed a bag, locked the house, and started out for the mansion. She didn't want to spend another night alone there and she was planning to warn Mable about her grandson before the police arrived. She would take the opportunity to talk to the staff about some of the plans for the future that were beginning to develop in her mind.

Chapter Eight

Arriving at the mansion she found the staff busy all over the house, and it took ten minutes to get them together in one spot. Mable had baked fresh rolls and made a large pot of decaf coffee. Cindy suggested they all sit at the kitchen table. They stood around and waited until she took a seat. She could see this was definitely going to require some adjustment. Having never been a mistress with servants, she felt a little awkward telling them to sit down. Under the present circumstances, she was happy to have an all-new staff. She would never feel comfortable in such a formal atmosphere.

After they talked for a short time, exchanging descriptions of their duties, she explained her plans for the house and grounds. The first thing she wanted to do was install a completely new security system and they would have to get used to having it in the house as well as on the grounds.

"It will probably be easier if the houseman is in charge of turning it on at night and off in the morning," she said. "Next I will advertise for help. I already have someone in mind to be my personal secretary and manager. She will also help me find a new staff as quickly as possible. I know you want to start your retirement," Cindy said. "I would appreciate all the help you can give her to make the transition run smoothly. First of all, I want you all to know I am no longer a suspect in Elizabeth's murder. The police believe they have the culprits. They will make their arrests known to the press as soon as they have them in custody and brought before a judge."

She wanted the staff to be comfortable around her and thought they deserved to be the first to know the latest developments.

"I know how much you all loved Mrs. Elizabeth and you can rest easier now knowing her killers are no longer at large."

The staff was dismissed, but she asked Mable if she would stay a few minutes.

Mable smiled at her but thought to herself, *I knew she was going to be a picky eater and I'm not too keen on having someone tell me what to prepare; but it shouldn't be for long so I can adjust.*

Mable had had the kitchen all to herself for twenty years. She sat back down and waited to hear what Cindy had to say.

Cindy started the conversation by complementing her on her cooking and saying she was sure anything Mable prepared was going to be fit for a king. Mable smiled and relaxed a little.

Maybe this woman, wasn't going to be so hard to please after all; but then what did she want from me?

"Mable, I have some news for you. First I want you to know I am sure you had nothing to do with any of what I am about to tell you," Cindy said.

Mable frowned and started to tense up again.

Cindy continued, "Your grandson borrowed my car while I was away and stayed at my home, uninvited, for several days. He and another boy were identified by neighbors. He left the day I returned."

Mable let out a terrible gasp and looked ready to faint.

"Oh, Lord," she gasped.

"That isn't the worse of it, dear," Cindy said. "He was seen here the day of Elizabeth's murder."

Cindy's last statement did it. Mable fell from her chair in a heap on the floor. Cindy got up and tried to catch her but Mabel out-weighed her by more than fifty pounds. She did manage to put her hand between Mable's head and the oak table leg. Her hand took a terrible whack, but saved Mable from a nasty crack on the skull. Cindy felt very sorry for the plump little woman; she was probably the sweetest member of the household staff. Rushing to the downstairs powder room, she returned with the smelling salts from the medicine cabinet. Cindy cracked the cylinder and put it under Mable's nose. She coughed several times and began to stir, trying to pull herself to an upright position.

"Lie still and rest for a few minutes; you've had quite a shock. I didn't want to tell you in front of the staff, but I wanted to warn you. I think the police will be here soon to question you," Cindy whispered.

Mable thanked her and again tried to get up off the floor. Cindy leaned down and attempted to help her rise and sit in a chair. Mable moved onto the chair and began to cry.

The doorbell rang seconds later and Monohan walked into the kitchen. He greeted Cindy and walked around her to look down on the pale maid, still trembling and sobbing.

"I've got to question you," he told Mable. "You might want a lawyer present," he said as he started reading Mable her rights.

"Why would she need a counselor? And stop that Mirandizing!" Cindy almost yelled at Monohan.

"We don't know if she was involved with Sam on the burglary or not; haven't been able to locate her grandson or his buddy," he said.

"Don't say a word, Mable; I'll get the attorneys over here pronto," Cindy cried. "They are not going to railroad you while I'm around."

She turned to Tim. "This is absurd, Monohan, just because you can't locate your prize suspect doesn't mean you can come in here and take it out on Mable. Do we have to do all your work for you?"

She knew she wasn't being fair to him, and she knew the caseload he must be carrying. They were always short of help at the station, but at this point in time she didn't like anyone from that precinct. His attitude toward Mable had upset her and he moved down a notch in Cindy's estimation, just when she was starting to like him.

Mable began to cry harder now. Monohan seemed to back off a little and sat down at the table. Cindy poured him a cup of coffee. He sat patiently and didn't say anything until Mable stopped crying.

"Do you know where he is, Mable?" he asked more kindly.

After calming down from the shock, Mable said, "I only know one of his friends," and she described the other suspect. "He might be over there."

"Where might that be?" he asked.

"Over on Sixth and Pleasant Streets. He and a friend live in a dirty looking, gray brick building on the corner. The boys have a workshop of sorts out back in the garage and are always working on someone's car," Mable said. "They do a pretty good business. They were here last month and Sammy gave me a lovely bottle of expensive perfume for my birthday."

Monohan figured they were probably casing the house, and went to the phone and called his office. He requested backup to meet him two doors from the building on Pleasant. He said good-byes and left the same way he arrived, in a hurry.

Cindy and Mable sat facing one another.

"Don't worry. I'm here for you," she told the old cook. "Officer Monohan knows now you knew nothing about your grandson's activities. Do his parents have any control over him?"

"No! My daughter is alone and has done the best she knew how for the boy. She works long, hard hours to provide for him, but it never seems to be enough to satisfy young Sammy. He has been out of her home for the last year, running with the wrong kind of boys, and getting in and out of trouble; just short of doing jail time."

She sat for a little longer and then asked Mable if she could help her find a suitable room for the night. Cindy knew most of the rooms in the old mansion, as she had done as thorough appraisal for Elizabeth; but she wanted to keep Mable busy. She wanted to keep Mable's mind off what might be happening to her grandson.

They walked into the bedrooms on the first floor. After finding a room that suited her, she said she would move in tonight. She didn't want to be upstairs because most of the live-in help had rooms on the upper floors and she did not want it to appear as if she were hovering over them. Elizabeth's rooms had been on the main floor and, Cindy reasoned, she should choose her room there also.

Cindy went to her car and brought in her small travel bag and started unpacking it for the night. She would bring her other things over later.

Changing into a clean blouse, she walked back to the kitchen. She had talked Mable into fixing them a dinner that they could share at the kitchen table. She wanted to stay near her.

Mable already had the small table set with two place settings and was busy at the stove. She took one of the chairs and turned to face Mable while she cooked. It was wonderful watching Mable move smoothly around the kitchen and carrying on a conversation at the same time.

"I could never manage more than one job at a time in the kitchen," she told her.

Chapter Nine

Back in town, Monohan and Tom Adam, another detective, pulled up two doors from the gray brick building in unmarked police cars. Two minutes later two more unmarked cars joined them, each holding two uniformed officers. Tim Monohan sent one team to the rear of the garage behind the gray building and split the other team, telling each of them to take positions on each side of the building. Tom and Monohan took the front, walking slowly. He knocked on the door but did not get a response. They went to the rear of the building and looked in the windows, but saw little. There were two cots and a television in the dirty looking room. Someone had tacked old ragged curtains to the windows, in an attempt toward privacy. Walking back beside the building, they picked up one officer and sent him out in front to watch in case someone came running out that way.

They again approached the rear of the garage. Hearing hammering and loud music inside, Monohan waved the other three officers over to him and told them to come in with him carefully, and to station themselves around the interior walls. He quietly opened the exterior door. Slipping in, they saw two boys stripping a late model Thunderbird. Their boom box was blasting out some unidentifiable language.

Monohan whispered to Tom, asking for the search warrant he had brought. The boys were making so much noise, they hadn't heard Monohan when he first yelled "Police! We have a search warrant." He yelled again waving the warrant. Both boys dropped their tools and started to run. One went one way and the other made a mad dash in the opposite direction. Seeing no escape and realizing all the exits and walls were covered by policemen, the boys quickly raised their hands over their heads. Monohan walked over and turned off the boom box. The room was suddenly as still as a tomb. It took Monohan a second or two to get his hearing back.

Sam began laughed arrogantly. "What's the big deal, we are only fixing a friend's car."

Monohan knew a strip job when he saw one and sneered back at Sam. "Sure you are, he must like pushing a bare frame around town. Why did you run if you have nothing to hide?"

"We didn't know who you were. Anyone can howl 'Police.' We had other guys try to muscle in on our little business before." Sam tried to explain the situation to Monohan. "We ain't done nothin' wrong."

Monohan walked over to where the boys had been working on the car. He knew the first thing they would have done was to eliminate the serial numbers, if they had had time. Thugs like these knew how hard it was to trace parts that have been scattered around the state. Turning around, he stared hard at the boys for about thirty seconds.

"You better shut your mouth before you dig yourselves an even deeper hole than you are in already," he said. "Read 'em their rights."

The officer nearest the boys obliged and Tim asked them if they understood the officer.

"Yeah, yeah!" Mable's grandson sneered.

The police handcuffed the boys while Monohan searched the garage for Cindy's stolen merchandise. He came up empty except for the T-Bird. The boys were put in separate cars and taken away.

Chapter Ten

The boy with Mable's grandson was Rod Smithy; he had a rap sheet with four aliases. Most of his crimes were juvenile petty theft, but he had served time for grand theft auto. He should have received a long stretch in the penitentiary, but because of his age, he had been released after serving only six months at a youth farm. Up until now he seemed to have cleaned up his act.

The boys were taken to headquarters and put in separate holding cells. Rod fit the description Cindy's neighbor had given them of the passenger in Cindy's car the day they were seen at Elizabeth's. Monohan knew from experience that Rod would take longer to crack than Sam; so they took Sam in first for questioning.

"Your friend is going to cop a plea soon since he knows it is a murder rap you're facing," Monohan told the boy. "The first to admit anything is the one who will be able to plea bargain."

"I thought you wanted us for stripping cars. I don't know what you are talking about. I didn't kill Mrs. Hargrove."

Monohan smiled. "I never told you who was murdered."

"She is the one everyone is talking about so I figured you want to pin it on us," Sam accused.

"Son, you don't realize you are in big trouble and you'd better face the fact. This is not going to be any walk in the park. This is premeditated murder."

Sam began to cry.

"No! No! It was an accident. He didn't mean to kill her," Sam yelled.

"Then you'd better tell me everything. I'd hate to see Mable's grandson take the rap for a two-bit punk like Rod," Monohan told the boy.

Sam looked like a scared kid and his tough outer shell collapsed. Monohan almost felt sorry for the young man. It took less than forty minutes for Sam to tell them all they needed to know.

"It was my idea to borrow Cindy's car and take it to the estate," Sam admitted. "I knew the old lady would let us in if we had Cindy's car. We planned on robbing her when she wasn't looking and figured she would think she had just misplaced or lost what we took. My grandma told me Mrs. Hargrove was doing a lot of forgetting lately, and Grandma was always having to find stuff for her. Rod saw the rings on the old lady's fingers and got greedy. He told her to take them off, and when she refused, he hit her and knocked her down. He took off the rings and a large cameo she was wearing on her blouse. He tried to get her to wake up to tell us where the safe was, but she just laid there," Sam started crying again.

Tim showed little sympathy for the boy and said, "Go on, then what did you do?"

"Rod kept shaking and kicking her. I got nervous and ran out. Rod ran after me and stopped me as I was getting into the car. He said the old girl was probably dead or dying and he wasn't going to leave empty-handed. He said no one would ever find out. He told me to pull the car in the garage. He was going to go back in the house and strip it of everything he thought we could hock. We made a few bucks on some of it, but it was slow peddling that old junk. That's how we got the Thunderbird. We traded the stuff for the car and were to stripping it for parts. It is easier to get cash for stripped parts than hocking all the junk we lifted from the house. The Thunderbird is worth more in parts than when it came off the showroom floor. We didn't know about the police finding the body until Grandma told me. She asked me to be a pallbearer. I didn't want to do it, but I was afraid it would look bad if I refused. I only got off the hook when the church said they already asked several men from Elizabeth's congregation." Sam stopped again and gave a deep sigh. "What's going to happen to me?"

He ignored Sam's question. He had taped their conversation and asked Sam if he had anymore to tell.

"Only that we used Cindy's house as a hideout for several days. Rod was able to bypass her security system, and once we got inside, we found her car keys hanging on a hook in the kitchen. After Elizabeth's death, we lived pretty good for almost a week. We cleaned up and started to move out of the house as soon as Grandma told us Cindy was coming home for the funeral. We really had to hustle. If Cindy had entered the house and not just picked up her car to go directly to the funeral, she'd have caught us for sure. Luckily, we left her car in the garage, so after she pulled out, we walked the three blocks to the bus. We been working in the shop ever since, until you busted in on us."

Monohan had the confession typed and Sam signed it. He was led out to be fingerprinted, photographed, booked, and put in a cell.

Monohan then went to see Rod. Sam's confession was in his hand.

"Let me tell you how this is going down," he told him.

He sat down on the opposite side of the long table, facing him. Monohan read Sam's confession and watched Rod squirm until he almost fell off his chair.

The cocky look left his face and he shouted, "That's the way it happened all right but Sam killed the old lady."

An hour later, Monohan had Rod's confession typed and signed. He would let the courts decide which one was lying. His money was on Rod as the real killer. Sam was just a pawn being used by a so-called pal.

Monohan called Cindy at the mansion and told her what happened and to have Mable get the kid a lawyer. He then sat down to relax a minute, wondering how some kids could make such a mess of their lives.

There were a lot of difficult times in Cindy life, but one of the worst was telling Mable about her grandson's confession. They cried in each other's arms; Mable for her grandson and Cindy for Mable. It was difficult to recommend an attorney for Sam's defense, since Cindy would rather see him hang for all he did to Elizabeth, but she had to help Mable.

The next few weeks were trying on the staff, as well as on Cindy.

Tim came out to the manor on Friday afternoon to tell Mable she was no longer a suspect and that they were finished with her testimony. Cindy had her flown down to the condos in Florida to get her away from the reporters and all the hype over the trial. The remaining members of the staff would fill in for her until Cindy could find a permanent replacement for Mable.

Chapter Eleven

On Saturday Jerry and his wife Jan visited the manor. Cindy heard them coming up the drive before she saw them. She couldn't miss the sound of a Harley. Mary opened the gate for them after informing Cindy they were waiting. Why they drove to the side door, Cindy didn't know, but she had an idea. She met them there with an admiring smile.

Jerry was riding a beautiful old Harley with its high tank and wide bars. A person had to have a long arm to reach the end of those handlebars. He smiled up at her and introduced his wife. She was on a smaller, chopped Harley, with a sidecar.

"You didn't bring the baby!" Cindy complained.

"Oh no! We have to ride double with a couple guys on the way back to the clubhouse. We're to call them and they'll come out to pick us up," he said. Pointing to the cycles, he added, "These are for you. They were the ones Mrs. Elizabeth gave us to use while ours were being repaired."

"No, Jerry, Elizabeth wanted you to have them; they're yours. I couldn't ride that big hog if I wanted to. Besides the sidecar will be perfect for your son when he gets a little older."

"But they are really yours," he protested.

"No! I won't accept them. Let's hear no more about it. Elizabeth meant for you to have them, and that's final. Now, please come in for some tea and cookies. You will be my first guests," she smiled.

They went in the side door and Cindy asked Mable's assistant to bring in some tea and cookies. The little woman looked questioning at Cindy, but returned to the kitchen. The three young people sat in the front parlor and talked motorcycles until the tea arrived.

"Have you decided what you will do with your share of the inheritance?" Cindy asked as she poured tea for Jan.

"We had a meeting with the club and voted to put it in to some stock. We thought maybe you could tell us which ones were safest," she told Cindy.

Cindy laughed. "Don't ask me. I'm as confused as you are, but I will put you in touch with my advisors and they should be able to help you."

"That's very kind of you," Jerry said. Looking at Jan, he smiled, "Well, come on, woman," he put his hand out to help Jan up. "We've taken up enough of this lovely lady's time."

He put his arm around his wife and Cindy noticed for the first time how tired Jan looked.

"Is there anything the matter, hon?" she asked. "I was surprised to see you out here today. I recall you usually clean motel rooms on Saturday."

"I usually do, but the owner put a couple young girls on staff who will work for less, and cut back my hours. I'd love to get a better job, but they are hard to find. I've wanted to break into domestic work for years, but it's hard to crack into an established estate. These old houses keep the same help year after year."

"Why don't you send me a resume and I'll see what I can do," Cindy told her. "I can't promise you anything better, but I'll see if I can find a place on one of the local estates."

"That would be great! I'll see that you get one this week," she smiled and left the house with Jerry.

Cindy waved as they went down the drive, and then she walked back into the manor. The dishes were already removed when she arrived back in the parlor.

The maid followed her in and asked "Will there be anything else, ma'am?"

"No, but you had better get used to Jan, she may be a permanent fixture around here soon."

The maid's eyebrows raised in alarm. It was obvious she had looked down her pointed nose at both of Cindy's guests.

"I'll be in my office if anyone else calls," Cindy stated and left her standing alone in the parlor.

Chapter Twelve

Monday was the day of the monthly board meeting of Habitat for Humanity. Cindy, an officer on the board, tried not to miss any Habitat function. She was not looking forward to all the questions this evening, about the trial, murder, and her inheritance. She was afraid her presence might interfere with the business meeting so she timed her appearance for just before it started. Happily, after the opening prayer, everyone got down to work and followed the typed agenda. The board meeting lasted only one hour, and then they opened the doors for the public meeting.

During the open meeting, she was introduced to a family that had applied for a house and had been accepted by the board the previous month. The young woman's parents were presently living with them. Her father Dick had lost his job down below in the thumb area of Michigan, and the parents moved up to live with their daughter until the father found work. After talking to both parents she learned that Nora, the young woman's mother, was an excellent cook and her father was a born handyman.

Cindy asked if they might like to work for her on a trial basis. They could stay for three months and, if all went well, they could continue and Cindy would put them on staff permanently. If they were dissatisfied and decided to leave, it would be no problem. Cindy knew from being on the board that the local Habitat organization would have checked their background thoroughly and would have any other pertinent information necessary, so Cindy felt comfortable hiring them.

She explained to the couple that a two-bedroom home on the back of the estate came with the job and that they would also have the use of one of the cars. The couple was so excited about the offer. They wanted to start right away. Cindy told them to come over on Friday or Saturday and check things out. If they were pleased, they could move in on Monday.

Before Cindy left, she wanted to talk to Leah, the president of Habitat for Humanity. Taking her to one side, she said, "I'm moving out of my little house and I wanted to know if you thought any of our applicants could use it. The house is about the same size as the ones that are being built, and shouldn't need many repairs."

Leah called her secretary over and suggested she get all the papers and a quick claim issued before Cindy changed her mind.

"Houses don't just drop out of the blue sky like this one," Leah laughed.

"Don't bother," Cindy said. "I'll have my attorney draw up all the necessary papers and get them to your title company by the end of the month."

Being a real estate realtor and appraiser gave Cindy all the knowledge that was needed to handle a transaction like this. "That will give me enough time to move. I'm not planning to take much with me, so most of the furniture can go with the house, if you want it," she continued.

Leah was so excited. "We may want to give some of the furniture to our other families. May we come over and see it Thursday? Maybe some of the others would like to come, too," she exclaimed.

"Fine," Cindy said. "I'll put a pot of coffee on at about 5:00 P.M., if that's a good time."

When things were all settled as to time and the directions to the house, she felt good that something else had been settled in her life.

Chapter Thirteen

On Thursday, ten board members arrived a precisely 5:00 P.M. Cindy was at the house waiting with coffee perking away in the kitchen. They were all pleased with the sweet little house that had been her first home. They discussed the furniture and decided it should be put in storage to be used for different families who may not have enough of their own. She completely agreed with their decision.

Cindy had all the necessary papers with her and the transfer of the house only took a few minutes. It took a few days to complete the transfer papers, after Cindy had notified her new attorneys. Cindy smiled to herself. Any other time she tried to rush a deal, it had taken her weeks.

"I should be out by next week. You can plan on taking possession anytime after that," she told Leah.

Leah said that would be perfect. "We have a family with two children that needs a home quickly. They are presently in an old converted gift shop. It is so cold in there that they have to wear their coats. The diesel fumes from the truck traffic going by chokes you when you're sitting in the living area. It is really terrible; what you would call 'slum land-lording' at its worst," she told Cindy.

Cindy could not understand how some people could take advantage of families who are down on their luck. The family had already completed their sweat-equity hours. Working on building or remodeling homes was a requirement by Habitat before a family could receive their own home.

After all the people left, Cindy had an empty spot in the pit of her stomach for the rest of the evening. She was happy for the family that would be getting the house, but felt the loss of old ties. This had been her only refuge since Herb's death. She knew the best thing for her was to move away from all those memories and try to start a new life, but it was still heartrending. This would be her last night in the little house. She sat and had a good, cleansing cry; then she was ready for the future, whatever it might hold.

Chapter Fourteen

Cindy moved into the manor on Friday and was partially settled when Hazel, one of the downstairs maids, announced visitors. Dick and Nora were standing in the front hall. She introduced them to Hazel as prospective staff members and showed them the kitchen and guesthouse. Things were moving much faster than the staff was accustomed to and they didn't know quite what to make of it.

Hazel went into the servants' sitting room and announced there might be a new cook.

"It seems her husband will be working here also. Don't complain about anything—she cooks!"

"It has to be better than it's been the last few weeks," one of the scullery maids said, and everyone laughed.

The little guesthouse was of stone and mortar, approximately thirty feet by thirty feet. The bedrooms were large enough for twin beds, dresser, and chest, leaving little walking around room. The small kitchen in the cottage was quite modern and had been recently upgraded. The wallpaper around the breakfast nook and soffit was a delicate yellow. It was a charming little home. The natural fireplace in the living room was spotted by Dick as he walked in from the front porch.

"Honey, it even has a fireplace!" he exclaimed. "I told her I'd get her a wood burning fireplace someday. This will be perfect for the two of us, Cindy."

As they were returning to the big house, Cindy asked "What do you think, Nora? You haven't said a word."

"We love it, Cindy, and from what I saw passing through, I will be very happy cooking in your beautiful kitchen."

Her eyes lit up and she smiled, "I have an idea. Why don't I prepare your dinner tonight and you can see if you like my cooking?"

"Sounds like a great idea to me," Cindy said, "We are sick of each other's cooking already."

She and Hazel had been sharing the cooking duties after Mable left for Florida. Neither could boil water without burning it. The staff complained they were losing weight; and besides, it was Hazel's turn tonight and Cindy wasn't looking forward to dinner.

Cindy started to show Nora around, but Nora said, "Why don't you just go about any business you need to do? Dick will help me get acquainted with the kitchen. When he is finished, he can go out and look over the cars to see what might be done to them. I'll have fun in that great big kitchen."

Cindy left the two of them and went back to her bedroom to do some unpacking. The upstairs maid was hanging up the last of her jackets.

"Helen, I didn't expect you to unpack for me."

"It's my pleasure, ma'am. You didn't have that much to unpack," she replied.

Cindy didn't know if that was a disparaging remark or just a simple statement.

It was the first time Cindy thought about her wardrobe since Herb died. *I guess I could use a few new things,* she thought. She would call the local shop next week and have them send out some new pantsuits. She disliked shopping and they knew what she liked. Letting the owner pick out her clothes and send them to her enabled her to keep from doing a chore she avoided whenever possible.

Dinner was simple, but a real treat. It was ham with a sweet sauce, squash, twice-baked potatoes, and cole slaw. When Nora served the potatoes, she said to Cindy, "Where did all those baked potatoes come from?"

Cindy laughed, "Hazel and I cleaned so many we had to use all the ovens and racks to cook them. After they were done, we realized there were way too many for us to eat at one sitting, so we tossed them in the cold pantry. We had no idea what else to do with them. These are wonderful, much better than when we baked them."

Nora smiled. "Waste not, want not," she said, turning around. She retrieved a beautiful pumpkin pie from the counter, serving it with cream she had whipped herself. She told Cindy she could do much better if she could get to the grocery, since there wasn't much in the pantry.

Cindy was surprised she had found that much since she had not thought to go to the store. She had been there every day that week, but today was the first she had actually been in residence all day. She had either been in town working, or seeing her accountants or lawyers. It had been a very hectic week.

"Why don't you make a list after dinner, Nora, of the things you want; and I'll call the store and open an account. You can charge the groceries to the estate. Maybe it would be a better idea if Dick would drive you to the store later, if he wouldn't mid. That way you can familiarize yourself with it and have them deliver anything you need at any time."

"I'd rather shop myself," Nora said. "I can get bargains that way."

Cindy smiled. *A lady after my own heart,* she thought. "Whatever is easier I'll leave it all up to you. Lately if I couldn't nuke it, I probably didn't buy it," Cindy laughed.

The three of them ate in the kitchen, laughing and talking. You would have thought Dick and Nora had lived there for years. The rest of the servants are in shifts in their dining room, next the kitchen.

Nora insisted on Cindy sitting in the parlor for her after-dinner tea. Cindy figured she wanted to prove she could properly serve tea to Cindy's guests. She smiled and went into the parlor. When Nora brought in the silver tea service, she noted the little cook had taken the time to polish the entire set.

"Nora, will you ask Dick to join me?" Cindy asked.

Nora returned to the kitchen and told Dick that Cindy was asking for him. When they walked through the doorway, Cindy rose and shook his hand.

"I see no reason why you and Nora should not move in right away. If you need any help, let me know and I will have some of the men assist you."

"Thank you, Cindy, but that won't be necessary. I am sure my daughter and son-in-law will want to help us," he told her.

Dick and Nora Hansen became permanent residents in their little guesthouse that very day. His son-in-law borrowed one of the estate trucks. He and Dick loaded it with their clothing and possessions and brought them to their new home. Nora and Dick were like a couple of newlyweds. They seemed to glow and kept smiling at each other. It must have been very difficult for them to have to turn to a married daughter when Dick lost his job. He thought he would always be a good provider and the head of his household. This position with Cindy would prove his worth again. There was plenty for him to do around the estate and he seemed capable of doing anything needed.

Nora went into the library that evening after she was finished clearing the dishes.

"I want to thank you again for giving us this wonderful opportunity to get back on our feet," she said. "Is there anything you would like before we leave? I have made hot cocoa and thought you might like some before retiring."

"That would be great, but please join me. We can have a nice chat," Cindy said.

They sat on the Queen Anne settee for over an hour, getting to know one another. Dick came looking for Nora and Cindy asked him to join them. He returned to the kitchen and brought in his own cup of cocoa. He sat in the large leather chair opposite them.

"I wondered where you were, my dear; I finished *my* dishes without you," he smiled.

Nora laughed, "I guess you caught me, but we were having such a nice chat. I must have forgotten we were to do the dishes together."

"I'll bet you did," he smiled back at her.

Cindy enjoyed their banter back and forth and joined in their laughter. She would have to make sure a new dishwasher was installed as soon as possible. Dick looked at the old one and wanted to fix it, but Cindy insisted on purchasing a new unit.

"I think that was one of the first automatic appliances brought into the house. I am amazed it has lasted this long," she laughed.

Dick told Cindy about his work down below. He said he had worked for twenty-two years in a large machine shop, building up his pension for retirement.

"I went to work one day and found the building padlocked. My boss, the owner, had gone to parts unknown with the company's pension fund."

Dick had a difficult time finding the same kind of work in their small town. It was impossible to find a job making the kind of money he had earned for the past ten years. He was told he was over-qualified for most companies and they didn't want to pay his salary to a new employee. He offered to start with less pay and learn any job they might have for him, but they thought he was too old to start a new line of work.

"I was so desperate I was taking any job I could find. My last job down state was washing cars with a bunch of teenagers. When our kids asked us to move up north and stay with them for awhile, up we came. We had nothing to lose and figured it would help both families if the two men worked as well as our daughter; and Nora would care for the grandchildren. They were having a difficult time getting out of their terrible apartment, but they could not afford anything better."

Dick was delighted when Cindy gave him the opportunity to support themselves again. Nora said Dick has gotten the old fire back in his eyes. They all laughed and agreed the three of them had made a good bargain. Nora cleared the table before she and Dick went out the back door to their house. Cindy locked all the doors and knew one of the first jobs for Dick would be to install new locks and dead bolts.

Chapter Fifteen

A clean smell of washed earth greeted Cindy on Wednesday morning. She thought of all she had ahead of her with the house and estate. The first thing she had to do was call her best friend Rene from down state before she did anything else. She had an early breakfast and called about seven forty-five, before the long distance charges changed. Just because she had the money, she didn't feel she should waste it unnecessarily.

Rene answered on the second ring as Cindy knew she would. Rene was also an early riser. They called themselves "morning people." If either was still in bed at 8:00 A.M. they knew that person was very ill.

"Hi, Cin," Rene said. "You're the only one I know calls me this early."

She could not understand why Cindy liked it way up north. She had figured that when Herb died her friend would move back down state where Rene believed she belonged.

"Smarty! What if it hadn't been me?"

"But is was; so what's up? You okay? Have you thawed out from the last blizzard?"

Cindy began to bubble with excitement. "I couldn't be better and we haven't had a blizzard in months. You wouldn't believe what has happened to me. I'll tell you all about it when you get here. I need you to come and see me as soon as you can possibly make it. I have a new address. Take this down," she said before Norene had time to ask questions. "2459 Wykoff Road—I'll give you the directions too while we're talking," she rambled. "When you get to town take Old 27 past town and turn left on Crescent Road. Go past the horse ranch about seven miles and you'll see Wykoff Estates on your right; you can only turn right. You will see a lovely park on each side of the road; drive up the road between the two parks. You will recognize the park on the right. We had a picnic there the last time you were here. Go through the parks and you will see the entrance to Wykoff Estates. A large, brass plaque on the right post indicates that you are entering private property—no outlet! Don't pay any attention to the sign. Go down Wykoff past Wykoff Boulevard, on past a large cherry orchard on your left. You'll see a long, black, rod iron fence. Ring the bell at 2459's gate and I'll let you in. Pull right up to the front of the main house. Got that?"

"I got it," Rene said. "What is going on?"

"I'll explain it all when you get here. I really need to see you, pal. Plan on staying at least a week," Cindy told her.

"I can be there next Friday. I'll call in and take a couple sick days I have coming, and a week of my vacation. I should be there about 1:30 P.M. We'll go to lunch and you can fill me in on all this business about your new address."

They rang off and Rene sat for five minutes trying to figure out why her best friend was so excited and wanted to see her right away. Cindy had been living up in "boonsville" as it was, and now it sounded like she had moved even farther out in no man's land. She knew it wasn't fair calling the town names. Crescent was a lovely small town, but if you tried to go any farther, you'd be going into the drink. The lake was almost on Cindy's doorstep before and now it seemed she was even farther out in the sticks. Rene always teased Cindy about the area and suggested that if she liked the cold and those winters so much, why didn't she go down below and sit in her freezer. She smiled to herself. *Well, there isn't any sense in stewing about it.* It was obvious Cindy was not going to tell her what was going on until she got up there. She had better call Matt and tell him she would be leaving for several days or he would begin to stew.

Chapter Sixteen

Cindy wondered why she had not received the resume from Jerry's wife. She had seemed so excited when they talked. She was going to call Jerry if she didn't hear anything from them by tomorrow. Jan was one of the first applicants she wanted Rene to check. If she agreed with Cindy, Jan would be on staff soon.

Hazel walked into the room and she mentioned these facts to her. "Why! She dropped it off two days ago. Didn't that little snob give it to you? I'll go get it."

Cindy knew who had taken the letter and was going to see that she was the first maid to be replaced.

Hazel walked back into the room and said, "Judy said she was sorry. It just slipped her mind. She hadn't even asked the girl in, she just took it and closed the door on her. She told us she will be glad when you find her replacement. She doesn't want to work with 'motorcycle trash.' When she came here two years ago she thought she would be employed by a lady. I want you to know the rest of us do not share her views. We know how good you were to our mistress and we realize how hard you are trying to fulfill her wishes."

"Thank you, Hazel. Please ask Judy to step into the library."

This was going to be tough on Cindy. She hated conflict, but she could not allow the situation to go on any longer. They would have to do with one less maid.

Judy walked into Cindy's office and stood across the desk looking at her.

"Judy, how long have you been here?" she asked.

"Two years and nine months."

"I realize you did not expect to have a new employer so soon, but I want you to know that I will not tolerate snobs in my home. If you can't work with the people I hire, then I suggest you find employment elsewhere."

The girl looked defiantly at Cindy. "I have two weeks of vacation coming, I expect to get paid for those two weeks."

"I'll do better than that," Cindy said. "I will give you the last three weeks remaining in this month if you can be gone by the end of today."

"Happy to," Judy said, taking the check Cindy handed her and flouncing from the room.

Hazel entered immediately after the young woman left, smiling at Cindy.

"First time you were forced to fire someone?" she asked.

"Yes! And I hope I never have to again."

"We will be happy to see her go. She complained about everything," Hazel informed her. "You handled her very well."

"I'm shaking like a leaf," Cindy smiled. "I guess I have a call to make and try to mend some bridges with Jan."

She called Jerry's number, but got his answering service. Leaving a message, she asked if he would have time to help her pick out a Harley.

Hanging up the phone and smiling, Cindy got her writing pad and started making a list of "things to do." She was ripping off the second page when the doorbell rang. There was so much to do before Rene's arrival. She wanted to prepare a nice room for her down the hall from her own. While checking out the remainder of the first floor, they found a lovely room. It seemed to be Elizabeth's private sitting room. A bed and dresser would not be hard to move from one of the other unoccupied rooms. She would get Dick to take care of it the next day.

Forgetting herself, she started to get up and answer the door when Marge the downstairs maid announced Mr. Blackstone, her accountant, was at the main gate.

Now what! she thought. She had always done her estimated taxes ahead of time, and they were not due again for several months. Cindy asked Marge to buzz him in and show him into the library, while she ran to her room to dress a little more appropriately before she went to meet him. She came back to the library and greeted him. He shook her hand and she gave him a warm smile. They usually greeted one another with a hug.

Blackstone came right to the point. He understood she had come into a large inheritance and wanted to know if her books were ready to be turned over to Elizabeth's financial advisers, The Simons Firm, whenever she was ready. He knew Simons handled all the old money in town.

Cindy looked at him inquiring, "I'll only have you do it, unless you no longer want to be my accountant, Fred; or if you think it is asking to much of you."

"Oh no! I would appreciate doing your books. It would really be a challenge. I've always wanted to get to know the Simons firm," Fred started to relax.

"Well you now have your chance," she told him. "I want someone I know and have faith in to handle my affairs. Simon's seems to know what they are doing, but they have had a free rein for many years and I want more control than they are used to giving. They seem to have been doing fine for Elizabeth, so they can still advise me, but I'd like to be in on more of the final decisions. I can really use your help. I realize you will be working most of the time on my account, probably 75 to 90 percent but if you could see your way clear to stay with me, I would feel much more at ease with all that is ahead of me. You will be working with Rene, if I can talk her into joining me in this latest adventure. You've met her, if you remember? She was standing next to me during Herb's funeral—the one who helped me get through all the preparations."

He remembered Rene and liked what he had seen. He was sure she would be enjoyable to work with since she seemed to be well organized at the funeral. Organization was a trait to which he was addicted. He told Cindy he thought they could work well together and hoped to see her in the near future. He was so elated at his good fortune. To be working on an estate that size and with a wonderful person like Cindy would be fantastic.

Fred and Shirley had been Herb and Cindy's friends for at least a half dozen years before Herb died. They were by her side every day during that horrible time. They still called once a week to see how she was doing.

Cindy thanked him for coming. She knew she should have called him earlier to tell him what was going on in her life. She told him she was sorry for not taking the time.

"It was only because I have had my head in the treetops for the past week. There is so much to think about and it has been mind-boggling. I feel I am still in a fog," she said. "Do you think you and Shirley would have time to come out for dinner tonight?"

"We would love to," he said. "I could hardly keep her out of the car when she found out where I was going—and I understand how confusing your days have been. Please don't give it another thought. We will do all we can to help. I'd better be on my way since I have a lot of work to do to organize my other clients."

He would have to turn over many of them to other firms, but he didn't care; this was too big an opportunity to pass up. He wanted to also catch up on estate taxes and much more, he had a lot of studying ahead of him. He thought of Cindy and the Simons firm. He didn't want to disappoint Cindy and act like a novice when he met the company executives for the first time professionally.

Chapter Seventeen

The weeks had flown by for Cindy. She got her computer set up and then went into town; purchased a new fax, copier, and answering machine; and had them installed in the library. She stopped by to talk to Leonard, architect and owner of Leonard and Association, on Wednesday afternoon; and went over what she wanted done to the old manor house. They were to stop out and check things over and get back to her in two weeks with some preliminary ideas.

Fred and Shirley arrived at 5:30 that evening for dinner. Cindy was waiting in the parlor when Marge showed them in.

"Wow! You've come up in the world, my friend," Shirley teased and gave Cindy a big hug.

Cindy laughed and returned her hug. "I'm so far over my head, I am beginning to panic. Did Fred tell you he is going to help me?"

"Yes—about a dozen times! His nose has been in accounting and procedure manuals since he saw you. He doesn't want to make any mistakes. He has never handled an account of this size before."

"Well we will be starting even because I have never owned anything this size before," Cindy laughed.

"If there is anything I can do, Cindy, you know all you need to do is ask."

Cindy smiled. "Now that you have asked, there is something, if you have time. Rene can't be here for several days, and that phone rings off the hook. I can't get anything done. I'd like to have time to just sit and go over some things with Fred. Would it be possible for you to answer my phone and take messages for a few days?"

"Say no more. When are you two going to meet?"

"Tomorrow, if that is convenient for Fred."

"Tomorrow is fine, Cindy, about 9:00 A.M.?" he asked.

"Why don't you come for breakfast about eight-thirty, and Shirley can get a good meal in her before the phone drives her crazy."

They all laughed and walked into the dining room for dinner.

The table was made up at one end so they would be able to talk without shouting. It had seating for twenty people and Cindy liked dinner to be more intimate than formal.

Nora served a lovely meal as usual and afterwards the three had coffee in the parlor.

"Would you like to see the rest of the downstairs?" she asked Shirley.

"I would love to. I have been dying to look around since I arrived."

"I don't know what is in the rooms on the upper floors. I have hardly had time to go farther than the staircase since I moved here. I saw it when I appraised it for Elizabeth, but I have not been up there again. One of these days I am going to take some time and browse around. I would like to go slowly over the grounds, too."

Shirley said, "You'd better carry bread crumbs to find your way back." They all laughed.

By the time Cindy and Shirley returned to the parlor, Fred was napping in a large wingback chair.

"Poor dear!" Shirley said. "He has been pushing himself all afternoon."

"Maybe he should wait and come in a few days," Cindy suggested.

"Not on your life. He got his last client transferred to another firm just before we arrived, and he is chomping at the bit to get started on your books."

"If you're sure it's not too soon, then I'll see you at breakfast," she said to Shirley as she woke her apologetic husband from his nap.

Cindy saw them to the door, then went to her office. She found herself nodding off around 10:30 that evening. She realized how tired she was and left for her room.

The next morning she was showered, dressed, and waiting in the dining room when Shirley and Fred returned. She and Fred worked until dinner on her books, stopping only long enough for a quick lunch with Shirley. By the time the evening meal was announced, all three were ready to call it a day.

Shirley said she felt the phone was glued to her ear.

"I made notes of the calls. I put any I thought to be important that you might want to answer first on the top of your spindle."

She looked over at Fred, "Did you get everything finished?"

"I can see already that I will never get everything finished," he smiled. "If I did, Cindy wouldn't need my services."

"Fat chance!" Cindy countered.

Fred was to go to Simons the next day and get back to her after his meeting.

She could not thank Shirley enough for helping her.

"You always seem to be around when I need you the most," she told her.

Shirley smiled and gave Cindy a big hug. When good byes were said, Cindy watched them drive off the estate.

The next morning Jerry showed up, driving a cherry red Harley low-rider. She ran out to meet him, grabbing her leather jacket on the way. He was smiling from ear to ear.

"How do you like this one?" he asked.

"It is beautiful. Where did you get it, or better yet, how did you get it?" she asked. "You usually have to wait a year for a new Harley."

"Two came in the day I was talking to the dealer and one was a low-rider. He said the gal who ordered them backed out of the deal. She couldn't wait for a new one, so she went out and bought a used one. I told him who might be interested in one and he laughed and said to bring it out for a look-see. Say, do you know everyone in town?"

Cindy smiled, "Mort was one of Herb's friends on the force. He quit just before Herb died. I forgot he went into the cycle business."

"Hop on and see how you like it."

She borrowed Jerry's helmet and rode off on the bike. Feeling great with the wind in her face, she circled one of the barns and returned to where Jerry was leaning against a tree.

"It's just what I need to wind down after a day of paperwork. Will you take it back and tell him the left brake sticks and I'd like the throttle a little tighter? I can be in tomorrow and pick it up. I think I would like to try out the full size model, to see which I like better."

"Don't you want the price?" he asked.

"No! I know I'll get a fair price from Mort," she said, handing his helmet back. "I would also like to apologize to you and Jan for the maid's rudeness. She was really cruel to Jan when she dropped of her resume."

"That's not necessary," Jerry said.

"Yes, it is. Tell her the girl no longer works here."

"Jan won't like thinking she caused her to lose her job."

"She didn't. I can't stand snobs and the staff was happy to see her go." Cindy assured him. "I'll see a good household gets her resume."

Cindy knew she would probably take the place of her dismissed maid, but did not want to say anything until Rene had a chance to meet with Jan.

Chapter Eighteen

On Thursday the security system was installed and the Wykoff sisters on the adjacent acreage would have theirs on Monday. On Friday the security people were to return to finish Cindy's work. She found another couple through Habitat for the sisters, and they were to interview them the following week. They seemed like the perfect couple for two elderly spinsters, and Cindy felt confident they would be an asset at Wykoff Manor. He was an experienced driver and she was supposed to be an excellent cook, besides having been a cleaning woman for years. She would know how to help Alice and anyone else on the staff. Cindy hoped the sisters would be as impressed with the couple as she had been. With that taken care of, everything was in place for Rene's Friday visit. She should have plenty of time to talk Rene into her plan.

Cindy cleared her desk and wandered through the lower level halls, looking into each room. There was so much she wanted to do. She hoped she would be up to it.

Please, God, help me to please you and those around me, she silently prayed to herself as she walked.

She would be so glad when Rene arrived. She had other friends, but none upon whom she relied on as much as her lifelong pal.

"Well, this isn't very productive," she said out loud. "I think I'll go see if there is anything Nora needs from the store. I could use a little fresh air."

She walked into the kitchen to find Nora making pineapple upside-down cake.

"M-m-m-m, smells good," she said.

"I've got one cooling over on the sink if you'd like a piece," Nora told her.

All thoughts of going to town vanished. Cindy walked over to the dish cabinet and took out a plate; sliced a large piece form the cake nearest her, filling the plate; and went over to sit at the old oak table.

"This is delicious. It tastes just like mom's."

Nora smiled, "I took it from that old green recipe book of hers."

"That old thing! Would you like me to have it copied over into a new binder? Half the pages are falling out."

"Mercy no. I wouldn't want to take the chance that something might be missed. I'd rather work from the original, but thank you anyway."

Cindy finished her cake, said her "thank you's" to Nora, and left for her retreat. She went up the circular stairway and sat in the old reproduction platform rocker. She brought one of her many cat books that she had saved through the years and started to read it for the third time. She enjoyed Lillian Jackson Braun's writings, even if she wasn't fond of cats. Reading until she had to turn on all the lights in the little room, she closed the book and went down to her room. She promised herself she would pick up a good reading lamp at one of the thrift shops in town. She smiled to herself; she might even splurge and buy an antique to go with the room. She knew of four little shops in town that sold some fine old pieces. She had wandered through them all for years.

Crawling into bed she said her prayers and the last thing she remembered was her reason for going to Nora's kitchen earlier and being waylaid by the aroma of upside-down cake. She was smiling as she fell asleep.

Chapter Nineteen

It was about 2:20 P.M. on Friday when the buzzer hummed at the main gate. The maid pushed the button that the security people had installed and opened the gate, went to the door, and greeted Rene. She showed her into the library. Cindy had told Marge earlier in the day that Rene was expected. Not knowing the exact time she would arrive, Cindy was deep in thought and had not heard the doorbell.

"Well, will you look at you?" Rene laughed. "I can see why you asked me to come clear up here. You always hated bookwork. What are you doing in this mausoleum, anyway? You take a new job?"

Cindy jumped up ran around the desk to give her friend a great big bear hug. She told her how glad she was to see her.

"I thought Friday would never get here. You'll never believe what has happened to me, Rene. Sit down and let me tell you. "You'll need to be sitting when you hear the story," she exclaimed.

Trying not to go too fast, Cindy told Rene the whole story: about her inheritance; the size of the estate; the money; and everything that had happened so far.

"So don't call our new home a mausoleum," she finished.

Rene looked at Cindy like she had lost her senses. "You can't be serious? What are you going to do with this great big place?" she asked.

"That's where you come in, hon. If you'll stick around, I'll show you all my plans. We can have so much fun getting this place back into shape. I am hoping to talk you into staying as my extra right arm. I'm going to need plenty of help."

Rene said, "I don't know, friend. I just put a down payment on a larger house and have been made head of the department where I work. They are going to have a fit. I only finished my training last week; that's how I got the time off. I told them I deserved it after the crash course they just put me through."

Cindy told her she could pay her twice her present salary; give her room and board; her own car; plus she would have fun doing what she loved.

"You'll be living in this great old mansion. You always said you would love to get your hands on a big old house to bring it back to its original glory."

Rene was astonished with what she had heard. "Not this big; it must have 300,000 square feet!"

"Not quite," Cindy said, laughing.

Rene knew she couldn't refuse her friend; a new job, a home, and her best friend, all in one package. She was crazy about Cindy and would do just about anything for her, especially now that she knew her friend had ahead of her. Her boss would just have to understand. She would give them two weeks notice, and already had in mind her replacement. She would go back and put her new house on the market. It was probably too late to get out of buying the new place.

Cindy thought this might not be true. "Especially if you forfeit your deposit," she told her. "I can afford to reimburse you. After all, it is my fault you're not taking the house."

"The realtor told me he had another buyer when he presented my offer," Rene said. "Maybe they will still be interested. I'll call him tomorrow."

"Why not call him now?" Cindy urged. "That will be one less thing we have to worry about."

Rene smiled, went to the phone, and called her realtor. He could not believe she did not want the house.

"I'm terribly sorry, but circumstances have changed and I won't be living down state. Would you check and see if the other people I had outbid still want the house?"

"Yes, of course. I don't know how the present owners will feel about it. The other offer was $5,000 below yours."

"Tell them if they will take the other offer, you will turn my deposit of $5,000 over to them."

"That is more than fair, Mrs. Ford. I see no reason why they should refuse. I will get back to you by morning." He took Cindy's phone number.

"I hope the other couple will still want the house. I can't back out on the owners now because they are planning to move into their new house next month," she told Cindy.

"I'm sure things will work out, hon, even if you have to go through with the sale; you can turn around and sell it again. It might put us a little behind in our work here, but it can't be helped." Cindy assured her.

"You are always the optimist," Rene teased. "What makes you think I would be able to sell it right away?"

"You bought it, didn't you?" Cindy smiled. "You are not the only person with good taste. You know what the realtors' motto is: There is a ready, able, and qualified buyer somewhere for anything."

Rene had three weeks vacation coming and might be able to work something out with her boss that would allow her to leave early.

"I'll stay with you a week, then go back down and start to get things wrapped up."

Cindy suggested Rene drive home right away to sell her car and pack anything she wanted to bring with her.

"You can store everything on the estate until you make up your mind about what you want to keep. There is lots of room. I can have the estate jet pick you up when you're ready and you can be here waiting when the moving van arrives.

Besides I need something from down state so I'll come with the jet and we can fly back together. How does that sound?"

It was almost too much for Rene to consider all at one time. "Wait a minute, friend, you hadn't mentioned the jet before," she said.

"Oh that! It's only an eight-passenger," Cindy laughed. "There are some other little things I forgot to mention. We also have a stable and own property in seven different states. We will want to check them out as soon as possible."

"Glory be! You do need help, or maybe I should say a keeper."

They both began to laugh and Cindy knew there would be a lot of laughter when Rene heard about some of her other holdings and her future plans for the mansion.

Nora announced dinner in five minutes. She had really outdone herself to please their guest. They had pheasant with raisin and orange dressing, baby spring peas with tiny pearl onions in a light white cream sauce, and blueberry muffins, still warm from the oven. The salad was mixed greens with little ears of corn through it. The meal was followed by a chocolate desert that should be called sinful, and coffee with just a hint of vanilla.

Cindy was glad she had told Nora what a special friend Rene was, but also that she shouldn't fuss too much. She wondered what Nora thought would compose an elaborate dinner if this was not fussing. She was very pleased Nora had gone out of her way on the dinner and she told her so. Nora asked Cindy if they would like their coffee and dessert in the salon, but Cindy opted to have it in the dining room, and asked Nora if she and Dick would please join them.

Chapter Twenty

Cindy wanted Dick and Nora to get to know Rene. They would be working very closely in the coming weeks, and she hoped in the years to come. They all sat at one end of the table and talked for more than an hour.

The first thing Cindy wanted Rene to do was to interview and hire a new staff. She wanted Rene to get to know Nora and Dick, so she could get people who would work well together. She also wanted them to help her modernize the kitchen and pantry.

Nora and Dick seemed a little shy having dessert at the main table, but Cindy assured them this was the way she wanted all the staff to be treated and would not stand for extreme formality. She didn't mind being the boss, but she wanted the staff to feel comfortable around her. She had found years ago that if you want loyalty in people who worked with or for you, treat them with the same respect with which you expect to be treated. She'd never had an employee quit or ask to be transferred, other than for personal reasons, on any of the jobs she held and, except for the maid she had just dismissed, never found a need to fire anyone.

Nora and Dick hit it off with Rene at once, but then Cindy knew they would.

She and Rene had the same outlook on many things. The only problem Rene would have with Cindy was her generosity. Cindy was very frugal with herself and her needs, but could be overly generous with others. She would give a bum the shirt off her back. Rene would too, but she would check him out first and make sure he really needed it. They made a great team.

After Dick and Nora went back to the kitchen to get a second serving of dessert, Cindy told Rene about Jan and the firing of the snobbish maid. Rene promised to call and set up an interview with Jan the next day.

Chapter Twenty-one

After dessert, Rene and Cindy went into the library.

"I want to make this whole wing living quarters for us," Cindy said. "Next to the library, I'd like a dressing room, bath, bedroom, and sitting room with fireplace for me. I'd like a sitting room, fireplace, bedroom and dressing room to continue on down the hall for you. I've already been to the architect and they are drawing up the plans and contacting a builder. It will be a mirror image of my suite, if that's okay with you?"

Rene looked at Cindy in awe and shrugged. "Why not? I'm not crazy. If you use the whole west wing, my rooms will be almost the same size as the house I just sold. Seven hundred-fifty to eight-hundred square feet should do nicely," she laughed.

"The only difference will be that I have a tower in the corner of the library that sits out from the side of the manor with about eighty square feet," Cindy explained. "I think we should add one on the side of your sitting room. It will balance out the castle look on this side of the building and give you your own personal getaway. I plan on having the same affect on the east wing coming off the living room, and another off the kitchen, but they will be just facades. The ones on the east wing are only for balance." "Yours will be finished and useful for a retreat when we want to get away from everything."

"We could just hide in one of the rooms upstairs, if you wanted to get away; they wouldn't find us for weeks," was Rene's glib response. "I sure wouldn't want your cleaning bills, lady."

Cindy laughed. "Wait until you find out how many servants it takes to run this place. Well, friend, that ought to be enough for today. Let's hit the hay. We have a big day ahead of us. You must be dead tired after that long drive. I'd like to start early in the morning."

"The drive didn't tire me as much as talking to you this evening," Rene teased.

"I'd like start in the wine cellar in the morning after breakfast, and I haven't been to see the second, third, or fourth floors with an owner's eye. I should check them out also," Cindy told her. "Your room is the last one down the hall in the west wing."

She walked her friend to her room and said good night. Smiling to herself she went back up the hall to the library.

Rene was hooked. She could see the wheels turning in her friend's eyes that evening as Cindy shared her plans. Rene had always been way ahead of her when it came to organization. How thankful she was to have such a dear friend to help her through all this. She knew it was not the job offer that prompted her to join in Cindy's crusade in restoring the old mansion, but the love she had for her closest friend.

"It was good to be around Cindy again," Rene thought, as she prepared for bed and turned out the bedside lamp. She was thinking about how they had been friends since grade school, later living through her husband's and then Herb's death. She had missed her more than she realized. It was going to be a challenge working on this estate this size, but she knew would be enjoyable, especially with Cindy around. She was smiling and there was a smile on her lips as she fell asleep.

Cindy turned out the light in the library and went down the hall to her room. The covers were turned back on the bed and a cheery fire greeted her as she entered the room.

I might get used to this after all, she thought. Dressing in an old, oversized T-shirt, she crawled between the crisp sheets and thought it would be hours before she fell asleep.

Chapter Twenty-two

Cindy was surprised the next morning when she heard the maid bringing her morning coffee. She must have fallen asleep immediately, probably because she knew she now had Rene's help and didn't feel so lost. She smiled, thanked the maid, sat up in bed; pulled her Bible from the drawer and read her Daily Bread. It was eight o'clock before she rolled out from under the covers; got dressed in her old sweatshirt, slacks, and tennis shoes; and left for the dining room.

"Well, princess, did you finally get yourself up?" asked Rene. "I've been sipping coffee and making notes for an hour. Let's eat; I'm hungry."

Nora came in carrying big, plump apple dumplings in individual bowls with a small pitcher of milk.

"I know you said you loved your mom's apple dumplings, Cindy. I hope these are half as good," the little cook said.

After her first taste, Cindy told Nora she would have thought her mom had baked them. She couldn't have said anything that would have pleased Nora more. Rene gave a large sigh as she ate her first bite. Nora was humming when she returned to the kitchen.

"If you think I can hire the rest of the staff to measure up to Nora and Dick, you have another think coming," Rene said.

Both women broke out in childish giggles. "You have another think coming," was an old phrase Bill Cosby had in one of his television skits about his mother's favorite sayings. It always cracked up Cindy and Rene. They used the expression whenever they really wanted to emphasize a point.

They were still laughing when the phone interrupted them. It was Rene's realtor calling. She went into the adjoining room and picked up the parlor phone. He told her the new couple put in another bid. He promised the owners the $5,000 difference and they accepted the lower offer.

"That is wonderful," Rene told him. "I'll be back in two weeks to pack up my little house and you can tell the new owners they can move in as soon as we close that Friday. I'll pick up the balance of my money at the closing."

She thanked him for his quick work, hung up the phone, and went in to tell Cindy the good news.

Rene had just finished telling her when the two had gone into the library. The maid interrupted to tell Cindy there was a call from Miss Wykoff.

"I'll always take calls from the Wykoff sisters," she told her.

It was Sylvia calling. Without any formalities, she blurted out, "Did you know someone's been parked most everyday down the street from your gate and watching your house? He's driving a blue Chevy with four doors, license JC24 something."

"I was not aware of it," Cindy said.

"I think we should have the police check it out. Do you want me to call?" Sylvia offered.

"No dear, I'll call, and thank you." Cindy said. After ringing off, Cindy immediately dialed police headquarters. Monohan was in and Cindy explained her concern and asked him to check it out. He said he wanted to come out to see her anyway and could be there in about two hours, if that was all right. Rene asked what all the calling was about. After explaining about the Wykoff sisters' telescope and what Sylvia had told her.

"I put in a call to the police," Cindy explained. "Monohan is the only officer who has a brain in that whole office. He was the one who arrested Sam and told me to get Mable out of town as soon as she finished appearing in court. He knew how fragile Mable's health was after the shock of Sam's involvement. He actually seems to care about people, not like most in that squad."

"My, do I hear a little more than you're saying, old pal?" Rene asked.

Cindy's only reply was "You have another think coming, friend," which set them both off laughing and giggling again.

Rene called Jan and would be meeting her for lunch tomorrow afternoon.

"I thought it best that I meet her on neutral soil." she explained. "I'd rather not let her know you want her here until I've had time to interview her. I sent and received a credit report on her and Jerry already. You can learn a lot from those reports. They look very good and don't have any delinquency bills. I also called a friend of mine and he did a quick police report on them. Both appear to be model citizens."

"You know best. I'll leave it up to you. You're the one who has to work with her. If you are this careful with all the applicants, I'll be more than satisfied," Cindy smiled.

Chapter Twenty-three

Within the hour, Detective Monohan pulled up to the front gate. Hazel buzzed him through and met him at the front door to take his light jacket. She showed him into the library where Rene and Cindy were absorbed in papers, strewn all over the large mahogany deck.

"What a way for two beautiful young ladies to spend a quiet spring afternoon," he said as he accepted the chair Cindy offered.

"Well at least you have one out of three right; we are ladies," Cindy replied, smiling.

After the introductions were over, Monohan got right down to business.

"You were right in calling when you did, Cindy," he said. "The guy in the car is a cheap private eye by the name of Sicky Nelson. He would kill his own mother if there was a profit in it. I'll bring him in for questioning after I leave here. He'll probably tell us who hired him if he wants to keep his P.I. license. How is Mable getting along? Have you heard anything from her? She is a very special lady."

Cindy smiled, "She calls or writes at least once a week. She is doing fine and Sam's mother is moving down with her next month. Sam's mom Sarah said she can't do anymore for Sam here, now that the trial is over and he has been sentenced to a long prison term. She might as well go south. She is a widow, as you know, so she doesn't have to stay up here. She can get a job as an R.N. anywhere. You wonder how two such sweet women could have brought up such a no account kid."

"Sometimes there is just no explaining it," Monohan said. "We run into it too often in my business. There could be a priest, a doctor and a nurse, all in the same family and they have one sibling who is an axe murderer, go figure! It doesn't make sense."

Nora came in to tell them lunch would be a little late. She was making bread and it was taking a little longer than she expected. She was using that new fancy breadmaker Cindy had bought her. Nora made fresh bread from scratch and Cindy was trying to take some of the load off her by buying some new automatic machines for the kitchen. Maybe she should stay out of Nora's kitchen. She looked over at Rene and knew she was thinking the same thing. They smiled at each other.

Rene asked Monohan if he'd stay for lunch.

"Only if you start calling me Tim," he said.

"It's a deal, Tim," Rene said.

"Would you like a quick tour while we wait?" Rene asked, avoiding her friends' frown.

"You bet, I've been wanting to see this place since the first day."

They had just covered the downstairs and started for the second floor when Nora announced lunch. The meal, as usual, was perfect.

"We are going to tour the wine cellar after lunch, if you'd care to join us," Rene told Tim. "We started to this morning but Cindy's allergies got the best of her. Nora told us to come back upstairs until Dick had time to clean away some of the dust and cobwebs."

"That sounds very interesting. I guess I could take the time since this is my day off. I had just stopped by the office to pick up my check when you called Cindy."

More brownie points were added to Tim's list, Cindy thought. *How many cops take their day off to check out a car for a couple worrywarts like me and Rene.*

They enjoyed a long lunch together, sitting at one end of the long table. It seemed very natural, almost like three old friends enjoying an afternoon together. Nora brought the light Jell-O desert and announced Dick had finished cleaning the wind cellar, so it was safe to go down whenever they finished eating.

When Nora walked in with a second cup of coffee, Cindy said, "Nora, will you ask Dick to look for a small table to set in the alcove over there." She pointed to the empty area by the one window. "Rene and I can have our meals there. It doesn't make sense using this big table for just the two of us."

Nora smiled, "We were thinking the same thing only last week and Dick found one up in the back garage. He has been busy refinishing it."

"Thank him for me, please," Cindy said and she knew that evening she and Rene would be enjoying their new eating arrangements.

"What a pair of jewels," Rene said after Nora left the room.

"Yes, I could not have managed until you got here without them."

"I for one am happy you will be joining Cindy," Tim said. "She looks better this morning than I've seen her in weeks."

"Thanks a lot, I guess!" Cindy laughed. "I'm in my oldest clothes and haven't had time to put on any lipstick."

As they were finishing teasing each other, the back door slammed, which was unusual. Rene headed for the kitchen as Dick was saying to Nora, "That manure jockey, who does he think he is? He acts like he owns the place."

"S-h-h-h," Nora said. "We don't want to cause any trouble. What did he do this time?"

"Well for starters, I was checking out the truck Mrs. Lawton wants to give to Habitat. I gave it a grease job and oiled it. I wanted to make sure there wasn't anything I missed, so I took it for a test drive. I thought I'd stop and see olla-manure-jockey."

"Stop that! His name is Steve," Nora said.

"Okay. Anyway, I was about to knock when he came out and wanted to know why I was so far out of my territory. He said he didn't need someone horning in on his job; like I would even want his smelly old job. He acted like I was spying on him and all I was trying to do was show a little kindness. He is so far back there by himself, it has to be lonely. We don't even see him at meal time."

"Try to forget him, honey, he is just strange. He is probably a loner and doesn't want company."

"Well, I think someone should check on all the barns back there. He has everything locked up tight as a drum and won't let anyone borrow any of his tools. He is very possessive about them. If you suggest he loan you anything, you have to tell him where you're going to use it and when he can expect its return."

Rene walked into the kitchen and apologized for overhearing their conversation.

"What seems to be the trouble?" she wanted to know.

"Nothing," Nora said, "we don't want to cause any problems. We will find a way to get along with Steve."

"Nonsense," Rene said. "I have to know everything that goes on around here and I need your input. You both know how Cindy wants things done and the type of people she needs around her."

Steve had come just before Jasper's death, and when Jasper died, Elizabeth let him have free rein over the back forty. The "back forty" was an old settlers' saying. The "front forty" would be the manor and grounds. The terms stuck in Rene's mind when she first heard them and, from that time on, she referred to the estate that way.

"Cindy wants me to talk to a stable owner down below and see if his son would be interested in becoming the new stable manager. I'll see him as soon as I go back down."

"We don't want to be the cause of anyone getting fired," Nora said. "Of course not Nora, but Cindy told me she doesn't like his attitude either. He is a relative newcomer to the staff, and was not included in the staff retiring to Florida. She also questions some of the things going on back there, Dick. She doesn't miss much. He rubs a lot of the workers the wrong way," Rene smiled. "We're going to check the wine cellar next. Care to join us?"

Nora declined as she said she had more than enough to keep her busy, "But Dick would like to look around some more, if you don't mind; as soon as he finishes a job for me he will join you."

Chapter Twenty-four

The three of them started down the stairs. It was dark and damp. The lights on the walls seemed to give it an eerie glow.

Just then Nora yelled, "Wait a minute? I jumped the gun. Dick wants to bring down stronger bulbs. He said the old ones must have come with the house."

The three huddled together in the dim light until Dick brought down new bulbs. Turning off the switch, he replaced the wall lights. Finding the two recessed ceiling lights, he added new bulbs to all of them. Reaching just to the left of the first wine rack, he found another switch and the basement was bathed in light.

"Wow, what a difference that makes, Dick" Cindy exclaimed.

"By the way," he said. "You have a hidden door behind the third wine rack.

I discovered it while dusting that fourth bottle from the left, but it was too dark for me too see much."

Cindy walked over to the third wine rack; moved the fourth bottle on the left; and the rack moved away from the wall about a foot. It didn't move too smoothly since it must have been years since it had been required to reveal its secret. Dick ran up the stairs and returned with a handful of Nora's lard. He applied it to the small grooves in the floor and the sides of the rack. Where wheels were hidden underneath, he greased them also. This enabled the rack to start moving away from the wall. He moved the bottle back and forth and made the rack move in and out until it moved far enough out into the room for them to explore behind it.

Rene was like a little kid. She loved mysteries and Cindy laughed as she squeezed behind the rack, telling her to wait for her.

There was a large wooden door that squeaked and fought being opened. With Tim and Dick's strength, the door finally gave them access. Dick took time to grease those hinges before opening the door further. There stood yet another door, with a combination dial set in it. It looked to be made of a thick steel plate and was embedded into the concrete. Tim knew there would be four walls of steel behind that door. He had seen other old cellar safes built like this one. Now how were they going to figure out the right combination. They tried several combinations, each person giving his or her input in the job at hand.

Then all of a sudden Cindy said, "Try 8-12-34."

Dick dialed the numbers and the door swung open on squeaky hinges.

"How did you guess that?" he asked.

"That was Elizabeth's wedding date," she said.

"How did you remember it?" he inquired.

"That's also Cindy's birthday; of course the year is wrong. She is only thirty-two," Rene said. "Whoops! Now he knows how old you are, Cindy."

"Oh! I knew anyway," Tim told her smiling. "I knew her husband and he was always talking about her. I also know her shoe size, height, weight, and that her hair is naturally red. I know her favorite flowers are roses and that she doesn't drink or smoke. He neglected to tell me there was a great face that went with that red hair."

Cindy found herself blushing and felt like she should know more about him. This wasn't fair.

He must have read her mind as he said, "I'm six feet, four inches tall; weigh two hundred and twenty pounds; wear a twelve-and-a-half shoe; I don't smoke; and I drink very little. I am four years older than you and roses are also my favorite."

Rene laughed and said, "You'll never be able to hide anything from this guy, Cin."

They all smiled, but Cindy turned and walked into the cavern behind the open steel door, a deep frown appearing on her forehead.

A light switch was just inside to the right. She clicked it on and the bulb still glowed. Dick replaced the bulbs and lit the entire area. She found herself inside a giant vault. There were drawers facing her; a table in the middle, with two chairs; and a coat rack to the right, with both fur and cashmere coats on it. The left side had larger drawers than the wall, directly ahead of her. She went to the end wall first and opened several of the smaller drawers. Almost every one held separate sets of jewelry. Some held pins, others necklaces with matching earrings. There were matching rings with several of the sets. The jewels sparkled when the light bounced off the walls. There were lights on all the walls. Dick quickly replaced all of the dead bulbs. The vault seemed to have the lighting moved to positions that would best show off the sparkle of the different gems. There were twenty drawers; most held diamonds, emeralds, pearls, sapphires, or rubies; some of which Cindy did not know the names. Each drawer had a note inside telling what it contained and an appraised value of each piece, dated twenty years before. It boggled the mind.

Elizabeth had worn only her wedding and engagement ring, along with one solitaire, that Jasper had given her the year he died. Cindy had no idea he possessed such a gorgeous collection of jewelry.

All Cindy could do was sigh every time she opened a new drawer. What in the world would she do with all this jewelry? She loved the pieces, but all her jewelry put together wouldn't amount to one tenth the price of what one drawer held. She decided she would have to come down with Rene later and inventory it all to try to find a reliable appraiser. She could see her insurance rates skyrocket. They had not found any of it listed on the inventory sheets that had been in Elizabeth's desk. It was so like Elizabeth to forget she had the vault. None of the staff had mentioned a vault, so it must have been built with the manor; and they were never made aware of its existence.

She went to the coats and checked them out. They were all for a person of Rene's or Elizabeth's size. The full-length mink would barely have reached Cindy's knees. She doubted if she could have worn any of the coats, if they had been long enough.

Until now the others had just stood dumb at the sight of what Cindy was discovering in the vault. Finally the tension of what had just been found sunk in and Cindy giggled. "Well you have enough winter coats for a while, Rene; you can't possibly complain about being cold anymore."

"And where would I wear half of these; to the grocery store?"

Cindy laughed. "She hibernates like an old bear when it gets cold. She only goes outside when you tempt her with food."

She next went to the drawers on the left and found they were filled with stocks and bonds. There were eight drawers, but again no inventory sheet had been found upstairs that these papers ever existed.

"I think we'd better close this up until you have time to get your accountants down here," Tim suggested.

"That's a good idea," Cindy agreed. "I want Rene to help me inventory everything first, before they get here next week. Let's go see what else is hidden in this basement."

They closed the door; spun the lock; and turned the wine bottle. The shelves moved back into place.

"Here is the key to the wine cellar," Dick said. "Keep it locked until you can put a new combination on the vault."

"Thank you, Dick, but I'm not real worried. We four are the only ones that know the vault is here."

They continued to look over the wines and found some very old dates. Cindy would have to have a wine specialist come up and look it over. She knew a wine steward from down below and would contact him. If he could come up, she knew he would go crazy seeing some of the dates; but right now she had enough on her plate without thinking about wine that had been lying around for a decade. There would be plenty of time to call him in the next few months. The remainder of the cellar produced nothing interesting, so they all went up for a cup of Nora's great coffee and cookies in the kitchen.

They discussed their discovery with Nora, and agreed it was not necessary to tell anyone else about the safe.

Finishing her coffee, Cindy smiled and said, "That was quite a pleasant surprise. I can hardly wait to see what we will find upstairs. I have a picture of the original furnishings and the maids said there are a lot of storage rooms up there with furniture."

Chapter Twenty-five

It looked like a small parade climbing the stairs. Nora and Dick had joined them at Cindy's invitation. Nora said she could use a few things for their house.

"Maybe a lamp and table for the living room, if we can find an old one you don't need, Cindy."

Cindy wanted them to know all there was about manor and was glad Nora had time to accompany them on their search.

"You may be called on to remember where we saw some of the certain items at a later date. I'm searching for some of the original furniture. Elizabeth told me they never threw much away, and for our restoration to be complete, we need some old pieces," she told them.

After climbing the stairs to the fourth floor, Cindy said, "The first thing we are going to do is install an elevator for the staff. Climbing all these stairs could kill you. How in the world they got things from floor to floor without one all these years is beyond my comprehension. Their leg calves must be as strong as tree trunks."

Rene had to agree she thought that the elevator was a great idea. "I'll get on it first thing tomorrow," she told Cindy.

The second floor also had a staircase at the back of the house, and was reached by going around the corner of the first floor servant's dining room. The same stairway led to the third and fourth floors. The fourth floor had one hall down the middle, with three doors on each side, opening into the hall. When they opened the first door they found the other two doors were not necessary since it was one, very long room. The other doors must have been used to move things in and out to the hall and then carried to their next destination. The fourth floor was not as long as the one below it. The ballroom below had a cathedral ceiling that opened for fresh air on humid nights, and took up about a quarter of the fourth floor. The mechanics for the ballroom skylight ceiling, were at the end of this long room. Dick said he would check out the mechanical equipment the next day.

"It looks pretty good to me at first glance. I'll bet it still works," he said.

"I want to see the roof when you open it," Cindy said excitedly. "Be sure to call me when you're ready to try it."

"She's crazy about anything mechanical, that or has wheels and a motor," Rene said. "Give her a piece of wood and she will make you a table. Giver her a machine and she'll take it apart and tell you how it works. She should have been born a boy."

"I for one am glad she wasn't," Tim kidded.

"And give Rene a pencil and a piece of paper with figures on it and you can entertain her for a week," Cindy countered, smiling at them both.

Rene gave her a poke and everyone laughed.

They found a table and lamp for Nora along with an easy chair for Dick in the first room they searched. The remainder of the furniture looked too modern to be of any use. They could furnish a half dozen houses with all the furnishings they found. Cindy made a note to call the charity offices in town and have them out to see what they thought they could use. There was not much sense in leaving it all up there collecting dust.

"If we leave all this furniture up here much longer, it won't be worth saving," Cindy said. "There has to be someone who can use it."

"We'll check around and find out, Cindy. It is sinful to just leave it here. I'll check our favorite charities this week and offer to deliver it in our truck," Rene said.

Cindy smiled. They always seemed to think of the same thing at the same time.

"Good," she said. "I'm sure we have help enough around here. Dick has a couple of trucks fixed and ready for use."

"I'll be glad to be one of the helpers," Dick said.

Cindy smiled at him and said, "I knew who the first volunteer would be."

Not to be outdone, Tim said, "I'll be the second."

"Let me know what days you're available, Tim. We should be able to deliver most of it in a day or two," Dick told him.

They walked across the hall and found it was just like the other side, except its furnishings were many years older.

Cindy shouted, "Look! It's the table and chairs from the old pictures of the dining room. Isn't this great? We'll get these down as soon as the elevator is installed. It is too heavy to try and get it down by the back stairway. They must have brought it up the front stairs when they put it away in storage."

"It had better be a big elevator," Tim laughed.

They found almost all the pieces belonged to the same period. Cindy thought it to be the greatest treasure they had found thus far. By the time they were through picking and pawing, it was near dinnertime.

"Let's quit for today," Cindy said. "Tim, will you stay for dinner? I'm not sure what we'll have. Nora, I hope you will just make sandwiches or something simple," she said, putting her arm on the cook's shoulder. "I'm bushed so you must be exhausted. You've been cooking a good share of the day, plus joining this treasure hunt of mine."

Nora smiled at her and walked out into the hall. "I'll have something fixed up in a jiffy. You all go and have some tea by the fire in the parlor until I get it prepared."

"I'll fix the tea," Dick said. "Then I'll help Nora get things done in the kitchen. I'm sure Hazel and her staff have set the table already."

Tim followed Cindy down the hall where she showed him the guest powder room. Rene was already in her room cleaning up, so Cindy headed to hers. It didn't take Cindy long to wash a little grime off her face; touch up her lips with a little color; and run a comb through her hair. She was out in the hall within ten minutes and met Tim and Rene walking across the back hall and up past the kitchen.

Cindy glanced into the dining room on the way to the parlor and, sure enough, the girls had it all set for dinner with even a third place for Tim. Tea was waiting for them on the small side table by a crackling fire in the old, homey fireplace. *What a nice way to live,* Tim thought, *and Cindy fits into this atmosphere as if she were born to it. Some lucky guy is going to have it all, if she ever remarries. Rich or poor, she would be a great catch.*

Chapter Twenty-six

Around six, Tim received a phone call from headquarters. A patrol car had picked up Sicky and was booking him for stalking.

Tim said, "He can cool his heels for forty-eight hours, and by that time I expect Sicky will tell me everything I want to hear and probably some things I don't."

"Why the name 'Sicky'?" Rene asked.

"He got that when he was in the pen. He was always sick and had an even sicker sense of humor," Tim answered. "His last name is Nelson. He is actually from a well-known family. His folks were very involved in Michigan's political scene and were great philanthropists. They build hospitals in small towns all over the state and sponsored cancer research clinics in a dozen other areas."

"That's the name of our hospital! Is that 'the' Nelson's?" Cindy asked surprised.

"Yes, they built a hospital almost every year and had a research clinic established across the street the following year. Sicky was just one of those bad apples you hear about."

The light was beginning to fade so Cindy turned on the small recess lights on the mantle and they sipped tea by the flickering light of the fire. No one said much since it was warm and cozy just enjoying each other company.

Nora walked softly into the room and said, "Sorry to disturb this pleasant scene, but dinner is on the table."

"Don't have to call me twice," Tim said, standing. "I haven't missed too many meals, and I sure don't want to miss any of Nora's cooking."

"I like a man with a healthy appetite," Nora said.

"I don't miss many of her meals either as you can see," Dick added, laughing.

The three went into the dinning room and could not believe the spread before them.

"How many are supposed to be eating all this?" Cindy asked. "You'd better call the rest of staff in here and we can all eat now. Why don't you set it up cafeteria style and we can all dish up our own? The staff probably want to eat in their own dining room, but the rest of us can sit wherever we are most comfortable."

Nora agreed and moved all the dishes to the sideboard. She went in and informed the staff about the buffet. They all lined up and filled their plates, taking them to their own dining table. This was about as informal a meal as was ever attempted at Hawthorne, and some of the older servants were a little apprehensive. Cindy stood nearby and encouraged them to pile their plates higher. They smiled as they walked past her and out of the room. She knew she had finally broken through although some still had reservations about her as the mistress of the estate.

Nora and Dick joined the rest of the staff in their dining room, and all the chatter and laughter emitting from the room made Cindy smile. They seemed to be enjoying the idea of a cafeteria-style meal.

Cindy, Rene, and Tim headed for the parlor to eat sitting by the fire. When Cindy had finished, she went in and called the staff in for seconds and then Nora and Dick served coffee to everyone, before clearing the dishes from the sideboard. Cindy suggested they let things sit, at least until they could enjoy their second cup of coffee with the staff.

"If you insist," Dick said smiling. "Come on, Nora, you heard the boss; this will wait."

Nora put down the platter and followed Dick back into the servants dining room.

The old grandfather clock in the great foyer chimed nine times and Tim said, "You will have to excuse me. I want to stop at headquarters on the way home to make sure our prisoner is safely tucked in for the night. I'd love to stay longer and keep you lovely ladies company, but duty calls. I'll contact you if I hear anything. Thanks for the great day; can't remember when I've enjoyed a day off more. We will have to do it again sometime." Cindy and Rene agreed it was an enjoyable day and walked him to the door. Rene handed him his jacket and the three said their good-byes.

As they walked back inside, Cindy and Rene decided to call it a day also.

Chapter Twenty-seven

It was around ten that evening when Cindy heard a knock at her door. "Cin, you asleep?" It was Rene.

"No come on in," Cindy answered.

"I couldn't sleep so I thought I'd toss something by you, if you feel up to it."

"Sure thing," Cindy said, knowing her friend had something serious on her mind or she wouldn't have bothered her this late at night. "What's bothering you, hon?"

Rene came right to the point. "How do you like Tim?"

"He's okay, I guess." Cindy said. "It is very hard for me to trust anyone completely who works out of that precinct."

She remembered the little cooperation she received after Herb's death. She also wondered just how well Tim had known her Herb. He might even know what case he had been working on when he was killed.

"I was first wondering how well Tim knew Herb," Rene said. "He might know what he was working on when he was killed."

Cindy smiled, "We should be twins, Rene. I've been lying here thinking of nothing else for the last half-hour He sure knows enough about me, maybe a little too much. It makes me uncomfortable. He had to have known Herb pretty well for him to describe me in such detail. We will keep a close eye on Mr. Tim Monohan until we know for sure what he is up to and how much we can really trust him."

"I agree," Rene said. "Well, we can't do anymore about it tonight, but tomorrow I'll make some inquiries. Night, pal; see you in the morning."

Rene returned to her room and was asleep almost as soon as her head hit the pillow.

Cindy spent another hour going over that night's conversation with Tim. She really liked him, but was very intimidated by all he knew about her. It wasn't normal for Herb to discuss her with others unless he was very comfortable with the other person or had known him a long time. Tim might have ridden a beat with Herb at one time. When you ride ten-hour shifts, you do a lot of talking to kill the time; but that still left a lot of questions unanswered. Cindy was glad they would be doing a little checking before she got any more involved with Detective Tim Monohan.

Chapter Twenty-eight

Morning came too soon for Cindy, for once.

"My, I'm getting lazy," she said to herself.

She always got up early to read her Bible; dressed; and was down to breakfast by seven-thirty. Lately it would be eight or eight-thirty before she sat down at the table. She hurriedly did her morning routine and rushed to the dining room.

To her surprise, Rene was not there when she arrived. Ten minutes later she came bouncing into the room, all smiles.

"Just got off the phone with a pal down below," she said before even giving her usual "good morning" to Cindy. "He is doing some quiet checking on our friend Tim. Don't look like that, Cin. Tim will never know. This friend of mine is not stupid. He knows how to conduct a discreet inquiry. He's a former FBI agent and did some work for my old boss from time to time. Let's eat, I'm famished," she said, without taking a breath.

"Snooping always gives you an appetite, Rene; you're really wound up this morning," Cindy laughed.

Nora walked in and said it was good to see they both always wake up in good moods.

"Not always," Rene said. "If you'd ever been with Cindy on a camping trip, you'd see someone who is grumpier than a bear with a thorn in his paw. We only took her camping once and that was enough. She didn't like the hike to the site any better than the tent and sleeping bag."

"Of course the rain didn't help matters any," Cindy interrupted.

"By the time we returned home, we were barely speaking. I think it was more like snarling at one another."

"That's enough," Cindy said. "You have to admit you got the point. I wasn't asked on any more of your lousy camp-outs."

Nora joined the laughter, "I don't blame you, Cindy. Dick and I took only one camping trip and swore them off forever. May I get you ladies anything else? How about more decaf?"

"Pour us each a cup, please, Nora. We will take it to the library. You might want to send in another pot of tea later. We plan on being there all morning."

The phone rang as they were finishing breakfast. Cindy was handed the receiver and Tim was on the other end.

"May I come out? I have to talk to you and I want to do it away from the station. I'm at the gas station on the corner, on a pay phone."

"Sure, I'll have Hazel buzz you in. You're just in time for breakfast," Cindy replied.

"Great! I sure timed that right, didn't I? Be right there."

Cindy and Rene went back to the dining room and called Nora in from the kitchen. Cindy told her Tim was on his way and that she promised him breakfast.

"I'll have it ready when he arrives," she said. "How long will it take for him to get here?"

"Just a very few minutes, so you might as well pour Rene and I another cup of coffee. It looks like we will be here for awhile."

Less than five minutes later Hazel showed Tim into the dining room.

"Why don't you have something to eat before we talk?" Cindy suggested.

Tim thought that was great and they would talk as soon as he had one of Nora's homemade cinnamon rolls and coffee.

"How did you know she had cinnamon rolls this morning?" Rene asked.

"I smelled them baking when I walked by the kitchen last night to thank her for dinner," he answered.

Cindy and Rene waited patiently, drinking coffee until Tim finished with his breakfast. He was on his third cup of coffee, when he smiled at Cindy and Rene in a little boyish grin.

He took a deep breath and said, "To begin, let me tell you who I really am. I couldn't say anything before, until I got permission from the S.I.C., a special investigating committee the governor established to investigate possible police corruption. Cindy, your husband was a friend of mine and was working for the S.I.C. when he was killed."

"I knew it!" Cindy cried.

Tim continued, "He'd gotten too close to the guys we were investigating and they didn't like it. They did their usual thing and got rid of him. We were and still are investigating the Nineteenth Precinct. Herb was our inside man."

He hesitated long enough for Cindy to ask any questions she might have.

"Please go on," she said quietly.

Tim noticed her face was blank and complexion pale but he continued, "Herb contacted us and asked for our help when he discovered the precinct he worked for was dirty. He was very upset and worried about you. He was afraid, with your active mind, you would catch on that we were trying to pull down a large crime ring. He knew if you found out, you would try to help and might get yourself hurt. You're safety was his prime concern; that is why he kept everything from you."

The tears began to flow gently down her pale cheeks. Rene got up and went over to her. She stood behind Cindy's chair and put her hands on her friend's shoulders. She didn't want Cindy to see the tears in her own eyes.

Tim continued, "There have been an awful lot of expensive cars stolen and twelve estates broken into in the past two years, without one recovery or arrest. Herb had already uncovered enough for my office to send me up here and put me in Herb's precinct, working undercover with him. We think Sicky is mixed up in it, along with half the precinct. The only guy we were sure was not on the take was Herb. He and I sat on several stakeouts, but had no luck. I was out of town reporting firsthand to my superiors the evening Herb was killed. Until I returned he was not supposed to do anything but run down a couple leads, but he received a call from one of our snitches and went out to meet him. He left a message on my answering machine at home or I would not have started looking for him as soon as

I returned. They would not have found his body for weeks if I hadn't pushed an all-out search. We still have not found Sicky's boss, but we are getting close. I'm only telling you this because I just didn't want you to be kept in the dark any longer. We'll catch these guys but, we don't want to rush in and lose all the head honchos."

Cindy continued to cry softly.

Rene was the first to speak, "Thanks Tim. You have cleared up a lot of questions Cindy has been struggling with, and a few questions she and I had about you."

"I figured you two had pegged me pretty close, after I left it slip to Cindy all I knew about her; then we had an inquiry regarding a cop named Tim Monohan. Luckily I was the one answering the call," he said.

"So much for discreet inquires," was Rene's comment.

"I didn't want to have a lot of secrets from you Cindy. I'd like to be friends with you and Rene. I really enjoy your company and would like to come out here more often."

"I think that's a good idea," Rene said. "That way you can keep us up to date on whatever new facts you find in regard to Herb's killer."

"I have to go now," he said. "As much as I would like to stay, I have to get back to headquarters. Things are beginning to come to a head."

Cindy had still not said a word.

"Thanks for breakfast. I don't need to tell you not to repeat anything I've told you. We don't know how many downtown are involved."

Rene had returned to her chair when Cindy started crying again.

She looked at Tim and said, "Thank you again, that explained a lot, friend."

"I'll let myself out," Tim told Rene and walked quietly from the room.

She rose and went back over to Cindy, pulled her from her chair, and held her for several minutes until she stopped sobbing. Both women soon left the dining room and went into the library. Cindy had been pretty quiet through Tim's whole discourse. She sat down behind her desk and finally shared her thoughts with Rene.

"I wonder what he is not telling us. S.I.C. does not get involved in simple thefts. This must be pretty big."

"Well, we will just have to wait until Tim can tell us more," Rene said. She looked over at her friend, "Gal, get that look off your face. We are not going to play detective again."

Rene knew she was wasting her time talking. Cindy would be snooping before the day was over, and they both knew it.

Rene left for her luncheon appointment where she hired Jan on the spot. She would start in two weeks.

Cindy was pleased Rene had been as impressed with Jan as she had been and would make a good head housekeeper for the maids on the upper floors. Jan's papers revealed she was management material. She told Rene she knew several domestics who would like to present resumes, and Rene encouraged her to have them sent directly to the estate.

"What did she say when you told her where she would be working?" Cindy asked.

"She was ecstatic and couldn't wait to tell Jerry," Rene said.

Chapter Twenty-nine

The following day found the ladies at Cindy's large desk. It was wide enough for her to sit on one side with Rene across from her. The two women were making out "things to do" lists to be compared at lunch. Rene had interviews scheduled for 1:30 and 2:30, so she got started on the questions she would be asking prospective employees. She made a separate list of things she had to do after the interviews. She needed to pack for her return trip down state and when she got there she had to figure out what to keep and what to bring back.

Oh yes; first things first, quit my job—boy, it is never dull around Cindy Lawton, she thought.

The interviews went well and Rene had a possible downstairs maid for one of the vacancies. She told the young lady she would check her references and credit report before getting back to her within the month. The other interview was not so promising. The woman was too puffed up with herself and Rene knew Cindy wouldn't be able to tolerate her, for even a day. By the time Nora announced lunch, Rene was exhausted and famished.

Cindy met her in the dining room. They compared notes and went over the afternoon's agenda. Cindy had been busy on the phone calling in some markers. Rene knew what that meant; Cindy was already playing detective.

"I'll make a deal with you," Rene said. "If you stop prying until I get back up permanently, I'll help you track down any leads your markers bring to the surface."

"It's a deal. I'll try to behave myself, but you better get back up here in a hurry."

"I know, patience has never been one of your virtues."

Returning to the phone, Rene finished calling the credit bureau, checking police records; and talking to the friends and priest the prospective maid had given as references. She was quite pleased with all the reports and told Cindy she would like to call the young woman and let her know she was hired.

"That's your job, Rene; whatever you want to do. She sounds good to me, too."

Rene went back to the office and called Alice Randy, telling her she had the position and asking if she could possibly start in two weeks.

"I can start sooner if you would like," Alice answered.

"No, I won't be back for a couple weeks. I have to go down state. Let's make it the first of the month."

Alice thanked her and rang off. Rene felt good about her second hiring and prayed she could do as well with the other fourteen needed to run the estate. She knew of someone from down state for the stables, if she could get him to move. Thinking about what to do back home, she realized she would have to stop calling "down below" home.

She was a boony now.

"What are you grinning about, Rene?" Cindy asked as she walked into the library.

Rene told her she was going to have to start calling herself a boony.

"You'd better not," Cindy said. "The people up here believe they have the best world anywhere; no traffic and little crime. I know under the circumstances that's a laugh, but usually we have little crime. We do have excellent restaurants, nature trails; and summer, winter, spring, and fall sports."

"Stop, Stop! I don't need a travelogue," she smiled. "I'm going to pack and get on the road. I've decided to keep my little car, though, so I'll be bringing it back," Rene said.

Cindy pondered this for only a moment and said, "Great, then let's fly down, together. I want to buy some new vehicles for here, so I'll go with you and check them out. I'll see if Dick has time to come with us this week. I would like him to pick out the 4x4s and a Jeep for the stable.

"Why don't you buy them up here? Wouldn't that be easier?"

"We only have one dealer here and he doesn't carry the model I am interested in purchasing. Any of the other car companies are a half-hour or better away. I know exactly what I want and a dealer down state who will give me a good deal," she told her.

"You are going to make a car salesman one happy fellow," Rene laughed.

"What if it's a woman?" Cindy countered and they both laughed.

"Then you will make her very happy," Rene said.

Cindy went to the intercom on the phone and called the kitchen. Nora answered. "Is Dick nearby?" she asked her.

"He is in the pantry putting in some new shelves for me. Just a moment, I'll get him."

When he came to the phone, Cindy told him what she planned. Dick asked to take Nora with him so she could see their other kids while down below. She could also drive one of the cars back and save shipping costs; then they would only have to transport two back.

"Actually we will have to transport three back," Cindy said quietly. "I'm buying a jaguar convertible. I've always wanted one. I even know what color and year I want."

"Wow, a new Jag," Rene said. "You have wanted one for as long as I can remember."

"I'm not dumb enough to buy it new; they are too expensive coming off the showroom floor, but there is a local dealer who has been keeping an eye out for me. He called to say he will have two used ones for me to see near the end of this week."

Rene began to laugh, "You'll never change. A spendthrift you'll never be." Cindy had enough money now to buy a dozen new Jags.

They checked with the staff and they said they could get along for a few days without them. In truth, the staff could use the peace and quiet. They were not used to two whirlwinds running around the house. Cindy teased them and thanked them for their honesty and told them all to relax for a couple days. Rene and she wouldn't be back for at least a week.

Chapter Thirty

The two women packed several cases then called Dick, asking him to take them out to the plane. He arrived within ten minutes and stowed all the cases on the top in the carrier he had installed for just that purpose. The one that came with the truck was not big enough to suit Dick and he told Cindy; the old rack had been put there just for looks. The women climbed up into his Mountaineer and headed out to the back of the estate toward the airstrip. The jet was waiting on the tarmac when Cindy, Rene, and Nora arrived with Dick.

They saw Stephen watching them from one of the barns. He gave them a cocky salute as they passed. Dick looked at Nora and frowned, and she smiled up at him. He took her arm and they entered the plane. They went to the rear seats and sat next to each other, holding hands. She was so looking forward to seeing the kids. Dick had to admit he was pretty excited, too. He laid his head back and soon fell asleep. Nora smiled and put her head on his shoulder.

The jet was in the air in only a matter of minutes. As they circled the field they saw two trucks enter the west gate.

"Do we have any deliveries today?" asked Rene.

"Not that I'm aware of, but there is always something to be delivered on a working estate," Cindy answered.

She went to the cockpit and asked her pilot Randy to fly over the entire estate.

"Rene has not seen it all and I want to prepare her for what she will have ahead, since she said she would hang around and help run the place," she said, and went back to the cabin to sit across from Rene.

They circled, scaring several horses and nearly topping a few trees, but Rene got a good look at everything.

"It is so beautiful," Rene said. "I can see why you could fall in love with it and why you need help to run it. It is so huge. This must be a perfect time of year to see it for the first time."

"It should be even more gorgeous when the trees are in full foliage and again when the leaves start to turn," Cindy said. "I have never flown over it when it is showing off its colors."

"I can't imagine how beautiful that will be. The fall colors must be awesome."

They sat quietly absorbing the day while the jet flew almost soundlessly toward Detroit. Among good friends it was not necessary to talk continuously. They always seemed to know what the other was thinking. After she saw Rene relax and stare out the window, Cindy went into the cockpit to ask Randy if she could join him. He was more than happy to have her. She wanted to know all she could about the jet's workings. Cindy had a small plane pilot's license, but had not yet been trained in jets. Randy told her he would be happy to teach her.

"That would be very nice, but I'm afraid I would never use it. I like your flying and already feel comfortable with you at the controls."

"It is always smart to have two pilots," he answered. Cindy had to agree with him, so she got out her little flight book. It was always with her and by force of habit, she started taking notes. As they flew over Flint, Cindy excused herself and went back into the cabin to sit with Rene. She looked back at Nora and Dick and saw they were both asleep.

"Have fun?" Rene asked quietly, not wanting to disturb the older couple. "I'm surprised you didn't want to take over."

"He did let me fly for a few minutes, but suggested I rejoin you since he was busy with the terminal, getting the approach routing."

They began to chat about their weekly itinerary. There was a lot to do in a week's time.

"We'll have to look into buying cabinets and appliances for Nora's new kitchen while we're down here, she told Rene. "I'd like to check on Braymore cabinets. We might as well get the top of the line. They will stand up to more abuse. Nora will have a lot of meals coming out of her kitchen. She feeds the staff continually as they insist on eating in shifts. They seldom all sit down at the same time."

"I thought Nora didn't let you in the kitchen anymore," Rene teased her.

"I'll ignore that remark—as I was saying, we can check and then we compare what we can get for the same prices up north. We should also look at some antiques in the shops in Plymouth's lower town. There are a few small pieces I would like to find for the sitting rooms."

"Sounds good to me," Rene said. "I love to shop with someone else's money. I wish we could still go to the Mayflower Steak house. Their scrod and salad dinners were superb. I was sick when they tore down that old landmark."

"You and a dozen others," Rene told her.

"Whatever happened to the preservation of historical sites?" Cindy asked.

"Progress, my dear; anyway that is what they called it."

"I thought we'd go to lunch after antique shopping. We'll call and see if Joyce can join us. She'd be a big help. I called her earlier and told her we would get in touch with her as soon as we get settled. She offered to have us stay with her, but I told her we had already promised Matt."

"No one knows a bargain better than Joyce," Rene said.

Old friends are nice to call on for help, especially Joyce. Cindy had known her almost as long as Rene, and considered her another wonderful friend. Cindy had been blessed to have so many friends. Most people were lucky to have one in a lifetime.

The seat-belt sign went on and Cindy went to the back of the plane and woke her passengers.

"My," Nora said. "I had no idea we were so tired."

"I think you both deserved a good rest," Cindy said, smiling, and then went back to her seat and fastened her seat belt. They started their descent. The landing was as smooth as the take off. They taxied to a small hanger on the fourth runway, arriving only four hours after they had hit the air. Randy stopped the plane and opened the door. There stood Matt. She wondered how he was going to take all the news she had to tell him. The skies were clear and the weather was balmy.

"It is a perfect way to start a new beginning," thought Rene.

Matt greeted them as they disembarked from the plane. He gave his mom a big hug and kiss, then turned to Cindy and hugged and kissed her, too. She was like a second mom to him. Matt was a super young man and Cindy's favorite. She had been there at his delivery and helped Rene her first week home with her new baby.

Nora and Dick were met by their son and his wife. Cindy, Rene, and Randy were introduced to them as Matt went to his car and drove it over to the luggage compartment of the plane. The next day Cindy was to make appointments at the car dealer, and let them know what time they were to meet her. They exchanged phone numbers and climbed into Matt's car to head for his home.

Chapter Thirty-one

Heading for his place, Matt said, "Mom, someone has been trying to get you for the last hour. He said he was a friend who likes Nora's cooking, and for you not to try to reach him; he will call every two hours till he gets you."

"Let's hurry, honey, and get to your place, I don't want to miss Tim's call," Rene said.

They were sitting at the kitchen table when Tim called an hour later. Matt answered and handed the phone to Cindy.

His first remark was, "Don't come back right away. We have a warrant we want to deliver to one of the ring leaders before we lower the boom on the station house; but we can't find the bum."

"Who is it?" Cindy asked.

"The pawn broker who lives on Knob Hill," he said.

Knob Hill was the most exclusive area on the western side of Crescent. It was not really called "Knob Hill," but all the locals tagged it that when it was first started, on one of the highest areas around town. A contractor started building estate homes on extra large lots five years before. The starting price on his homes was $250,000, and if you wanted extras, it could climb up to several hundred thousand dollars more. He soon found out the old money in town would not pay his prices, so he started building more reasonable priced homes. The pawnbroker was one of the few that had built an expensive residence and was now stuck with it.

"Let me talk to him, Cindy," Matt interrupted.

She said good-bye to Tim, and handed the phone back to Matt.

"Matt Ford here," he said to Tim. "Rene's my mom. I have something I think you should know. I've been watching out the window for the past hour and some guy I saw at the airport has been sitting in a red Caddy outside my house. It looks like he's casing the place, and I am sure he followed us here."

"What's he look like, Matt?" Tim asked.

"Dark complexion, small beard, heavy glasses, business suit and felt hat."

"You just described the guy we are looking for, Matt; that's Sicky's uncle, Tom

Hastings. Do you have a gun?" Matt answered in the affirmative and told Tim he also knew how to use it.

"Good," Tim said. "I will call the local police and have them pick him up and hold him until I can get there. I'll get back to you in ten minutes. In the meantime, load your gun and sit tight; stay away from the windows."

Ten minutes later Tim called back.

"The local police are going to try to surround your block with unmarked cars and approach him on foot. If he comes to your door before they are ready, don't let him enter. He has to be sure Cindy is with you and he might try to get in. Now give me a description of what you're wearing, Matt, I don't want the locals making any mistakes."

Matt said, "I'm wearing blue jeans, jean shirt, gray 101s; and I'm going in right now and shave off my beard, he laughed. I don't want them mistaking me for the crook either. When I described him, he sounded an awful lot like me."

"Good idea, but hurry, Matt," Tim said.

Matt had just finished shaving when there was a knock at the door. He looked out to see a bearded man with thick glasses trying to look in at the small window in the door. Matt held the gun to his side; took off the safety; put a bullet in the chamber; and opened the door until the chain tightened.

"May I help you?" he said.

"I'm looking for a Mrs. Carol Anne Finch; she lives somewhere on this block," Hastings said.

"Well she doesn't live here," Matt answered. "Try the house three doors down. I think a Carol lives there."

Hastings tried to look into the room, but Matt was blocking his view.

"May I use your phone? I have her number," Tom said.

The women had gone into Matt's bedroom before he opened the door.

"No, I'm busy right now," Matt said. "She has to be the one three doors down, try there."

Tom thanked him and walked down the street before returning to his car. Matt closed and locked the door.

By then the police had cordoned off the block and two plain clothed officers approached the red Caddy as Hastings was about to unlock the car door.

"Keep your hands in plain sight and don't move. This is the police," the officer on the drivers' side said, producing a badge.

Tom gave no resistance. They handcuffed him and put him in one of the unmarked cars. While he was sitting there the other officer read him his rights.

"I've done nothing," Tom said. "What's this all about?"

"Stalking," the officer said.

"I was merely trying to locate a friend's house," Hastings told the officer. "Can't any of you guys come up with anything better than stalking?"

"Not that will hold you long enough for your local police to arrive," he said.

Tom grinned, "Local police, ha!" *I'll be out an hour after my friends get here,* he thought to himself. He sat back and relaxed as they drove him to the local lockup.

Chapter Thirty-two

Five hours later Tom's smile disappeared when Tim entered.

"Where is Sam or Fred? They should be here, not you," Tom demanded.

"I'm all by myself," Tim answered. "I forgot to tell anyone else you were here."

"Do you know who I am?" Tom demanded. "I own half your town and I don't appreciate this kind of treatment."

Tim sneered back at him and remarked, "I know who you are and you're lucky you are talking to me first, before I let Sicky know I've got his boss under lock and key. You know he'll cop a plea, so it looks like I'm your only chance. If you want to give me names and proof, I may be able to get you a lighter sentence. There have been at least two murders while your underlings have been stealing all that merchandise you've been fencing."

"You have no proof I'm involved with any of that," Tom shouted at Tim.

"I wouldn't fly all the way down here if I didn't," Tim told him. "We have a warrant to search your business and residence and they are being served as we speak."

"How did you get a warrant to search my place? Judge Thompson wouldn't dare give you any warrants."

"We didn't think he would, that's why the S.I.C. became involved; and what would you say if I told you we got the warrants through the FBI?" Tim smiled sweetly at Hastings.

"Don't tell me they are involved, too," he said almost in a whisper.

"Okay I won't," said Tim, "but you're going to take a big fall all by yourself if you don't open up pretty darn quick."

Tim was bluffing, the FBI wasn't involved yet, but Tom didn't know that. He was still playing society swell, and Tim was rapidly losing his patience.

"Of course I can always get you on the stalking charge and keep you incognito down here. I wonder what they will all think when we start arresting half the city and good old Tom is nowhere to be found."

"They will go after my family you creep," Tom said.

"You should have thought of them when you started masterminding all those robberies that led to two murders. You better hurry and make up your mind if you want to save them and yourself. I don't care one way or the other. Someone will cop a plea within the next few hours anyway."

"Okay you win," Tom said. "What do you want to know and what can you do for me?"

"We want names, places, and dates. Then I'll try to help you get a reduced sentence."

"No deal!" Tim yelled "I need to be in protective custody."

"Forget it, Hastings, there is no way you're going to get off that easy."

"There will be when you find out who all is involved and the proof I can hand you," Hastings answered.

He knew he was really in trouble. How was he going to save his own neck? This guy knew too much and he wasn't going to take a bribe, that he knew. Too bad he hadn't had him eliminated when Sicky suggested it. The little creep had finally had a good idea and he had ignored him; probably the only bright thought Sicky had ever had. There wasn't anything he could do but cooperate now. He knew the others would throw him to the wolves if they were given half a chance.

"Let's talk," Hastings said.

"I'll record our conversation," Tim told him. "If that is okay."

"Sure, why not?" Tom answered, straightening his collar and smoothing his hair.

Tim turned on the video camera and started recording. They were still talking two hours later. Tim was glad he had it all on tape. He couldn't have written fast enough to keep up with all Hastings had to say. It was bigger than Tim had thought when he arrived. He called the attorney general of the state and the governor and made them aware of the developments thus far. He was to meet them at the capital the next day. Tim had all the tapes transcribed by a typist and the copies signed by Tom before evening. He then had Hastings taken to a safe house, and assigned four S.I.C. agents to guard him around the clock. He called Cindy and told her everything was beginning to fall into place.

"I'll get back to you as soon as I can. Please stay where you are until you hear from me."

Chapter Thirty-three

The meeting with the governor was set for ten that morning and Tim was waiting outside the governor's door at 9:45. Governor Sam Thompson greeted Tim personally, shook his hand, and showed him a seat in his office by the fire.

The governor seated himself across from Tim and asked politely, "Would you like coffee or tea? I know how rushed you must have been to get here on time. I hope you had breakfast."

He did not wait for Tim to answer, but asked his secretary to bring in coffee for three.

"The attorney general will be joining us shortly," the governor said. "When he gets here I don't want any interruptions until I call you, is that clear?"

"Yes, sir!" she replied and went out leaving the door ajar.

The governor turned back to Tim, "I've heard great things about you and the job you're doing. I am here to help in any way I can. What do you need?"

"You can ask the attorney general to declare Marshal Law in my town and get warrants for all the persons on this list," Tim answered politely, handing him a sheet of paper.

As the governor looked it over he gave a long whistle.

"Some of these people I know personally. Several campaigned for me. Are you certain of your facts? Do you have proof that will stand up in court?"

At that moment the attorney general walked in the door.

"If Tim says those are the guilty parties, you can bet your re-election he has all the proof necessary," was his remark.

Tim answered in a quiet, serious tone, "I didn't look into this as a politician. I know you may be hurt by some of these arrests, but think how it will look if we only arrest the underlings."

"I know," the governor said, "I have no intention of just doing half a house cleaning." He had an edge to his voice. "I just want you to be sure of your facts. These are some pretty influential members of our state."

"Yes, sir, I realize that." Tim handed him the videotapes and written confession. "You'd better look at these, Governor, before we go any further." Tim handed the video to him along with the confession from Hastings. The governor wasn't going to like it and Tim wished he could leave the room while he viewed it. He liked the governor and knew this was going to be one of the hardest things he had ever had to do.

The attorney general took the tape from the governor, inserted it into the VCR, and walked over to lock the door. He pushed the play button and Hastings' face came into view.

Chapter Thirty-four

While they were reviewing the tapes, things were happening up north where a late meeting was going on in the chief's office at police headquarters. Everyone there had been attempting to find Tom Hastings. He seemed to have disappeared.

"It is not like him to leave and not tell anyone where he was going," one man said. "His wife couldn't shed any light on the subject either. He probably has a girlfriend stashed someplace."

They all agreed. He had disappeared before to be with some girl, but never more than one night. They wouldn't start worrying about the old fool unless he was still missing tomorrow. They were there to discuss more important things.

A message came in from the big boss, that an estate out in Wykoff was going to be empty, except for a few staff members, for a week or more. They could get in and take their time rifling through all the good stuff from the place. It was to be their last job, and they were to see it executed immediately. The cook and chauffeur had left and most of the staff were also leaving for the weekend. They would only have three live-ins to eliminate. This would be their biggest haul yet. They would lay low after this one for a couple months, and then take turns retiring to some place warm. A layout map of the estate lay open on the desk, and they were determining the best time to enter. The west gate of the estate would be left unlocked, for easy access; that only left them to figure out a way to get into the house without causing too big a fuss.

Two hours later they agreed to meet the next afternoon and go over their final plans. The chief was to have three trucks and handpicked men to drive them, ready at a moment's notice.

"I'll bring a half dozen extra guys to help move the loot," he said, smiling.

Chapter Thirty-five

Back at the governor's office three men were seated around a tape recorder. The first picture and voice on the tape was Hastings talking to Tim. Tim was reading Sicky's confession to Tom. He showed it to the camera and had Tom verbally verify the signature as Sicky's. Tom's voice cracked as he began to talk.

The governor exclaimed, "Holy cow! That's Tom Hastings, and he is accusing my brother-in-law, Judge Harry Thompson, of being involved in this mess. You'd better be sure of your facts, young man," the governor scowled at Tim. "My brother-in-law has been a pillar of this state for many years."

"I warned you, sir, that you weren't going to like this meeting," the attorney general interrupted.

The governor answered him, using the attorney general's nickname. "Benny, what are we going to do?" he said, as he put his hands over his face. "My own brother-in-law. What will this do to my sister and her family?"

"I don't think you have any choice sir. You asked for a secret investigation when this was first brought to your attention," Benny said. "I don't see what else we can do but get the warrants served and declare Marshall Law up there until we clean house and appoint a new mayor, assistant D.A., chief of police; and, sorry, sir, a new judge."

The governor put his head in his hands again and moaned, "What a nightmare." Straightening up he looked at Tim and said, "You have done a good job, Tim, maybe too good."

He added, finally able to give both men a weak smile. "I don't know how this is going to effect my next term, but you can be sure it will be cleared up before the end of this one. Benny, you take over. You know what has to be done. I'll handle any fallout at this end. I want you up there tonight, warrants in hand; and don't go alone. I'll call out the national guard for assistance."

He thanked Tim again for a fine job and left to let Tim and Attorney General Benjamin make their arrangements.

"I hate to see the governor put in such a position," Tim said.

"He's a strong man, he can take the heat," Benny answered. "I think he just wants to be left alone for awhile."

Going to the outer office, Tim called Cindy at Matt's and informed her of the situation.

"I wouldn't return for at least a week if I were you two. We are going to be very busy up there. You have done a fine job helping clear up this mess, Cindy, and we thank you; but now we have to do our end of the job."

Cindy told him to be careful and to please call her again when he found the time.

The attorney general entered as Tim hung up the phone.

"I would like you to accept the chief's job, Tim, even if you only take it temporarily. You know who we can trust up there and who are borderline. I don't want anyone left tomorrow but people we can trust.

"As long as you realize it is temporary. I'll be glad to help out all I can," Tim replied. "I will take a years leave from the S.I.C., I'm sure they will understand. We have spent so much time already on this case. They will want to make sure we have a decent squad in force up there before they pull me back."

Chapter Thirty-six

The afternoon was so busy that the attorney general and Tim missed lunch and dinner. At nine that evening, the plane was ready for them at the airport and a cargo plane commandeered for the job was loaded with national guard. They were to pick up more National Guardsmen at the airport upon their arrival at their destination. They would be coming up from Grayling, where they were on maneuvers. The Grayling guard would have several trucks available for transportation.

The two men had a quick sandwich and lots of coffee on the flight north. Neither said very much since they both knew they would get little sleep the next few days. Tim hadn't slept much in forty-eight hours so he decided to take a short nap.

The plane landed at a little after midnight and they climbed into one of the waiting army trucks with the dozen men they brought with them; heading for town, about fifty miles away.

Their first stop would be police headquarters. Walking in they found the Assistant D.A. Fred Price, and the chief of police, Sam Anderson, in Sam's office. They weren't expecting Tim and the attorney general to walk in with six armed soldiers.

"What in blazes is this?" the D.A. yelled.

Benny introduced himself and said, "We have arrest warrants for both of you. Read them their rights, Tim, and lock em up."

Fred and Sam both glared at Tim.

"What is this all about? This guy works for me," Sam howled, pointing a finger at Tim.

"You'll hear all the charges in the morning before the judge; right now Tim works for me," Benny said.

Sam and Fred both smiled. There was only one judge in town right now, and they knew he was on their payroll.

"Oh well! I need a good night's sleep," Sam said with a smirk, "Come on, Fred, maybe we'll get adjoining cells and get in some poker."

Both were taking it like a big joke.

"We'll make it easy for you," Tim smiled. "You can share one of the isolation cells at the back so your game won't be interrupted." Tim knew they would be receiving a rude awakening in the morning.

He started searching the chief's desk. Giving a low whistle as he spotted a map lying on the top.

"Looks like we got here just in time to save Cindy's estate."

The plans had been left open on the desk when the chief and D.A. were led away. "They were planning a real haul," he said to Benny.

Their next stop would be the mayor's home. Mayor J.P. Anthony III was having a dinner party and most of the guests were about to depart as Tim and Benny arrived with armed men.

"Welcome, sir! You're a little late for dinner, but come on in and have a drink," he said to the attorney general. They had previously met at several mayor conventions in Detroit.

"This is not a social call," Benny said, as the mayor noticed the armed men following Tim. "We are here to arrest you. I have a warrant issued by the governor. Please come with us quietly."

The mayor looked like he had been struck by a hammer. His face crumbled and his eyes began to water. "You actually have a warrant for my arrest? Whatever for?"

When Benny didn't answer, he turned and said something to his wife. Then he calmly got his coat from the front hall closet. One of the soldiers stepped forward and searched the coat, producing a .45 magnum from the inside pocket. J.P. didn't say a word after that. Handcuffed, he was led out to a waiting car. His wife was already on the phone trying to get their attorney, the district attorney.

They dropped the mayor off at the jail and saw that he was put in a cell far from the other two. By this time, Tim had chosen four uniformed police he could trust to help the national guard take over the jail and headquarters.

Judge Thompson's was the next stop. It was after two that morning and they still had his arrest warrant to present. Tim understood why they went for the judge's last. Benny knew him as a friend and because he was the brother-in-law of the governor.

What is on Benny's mind? Tim wondered to himself. It had to be the toughest arrest he was ever required to make.

They approached the outer gate of the Thompson's beautiful home.

Why did some people turn bad when they already had it all? Tim mused.

They were buzzed in as soon as Benny announced who was at their gate. The governor's sister answered the door herself with a look of alarm. "What is it—is it one of the children—is my brother hurt?" she cried.

"No dear, it's almost as bad," Benny told her. "We came to arrest the judge."

"Oh no!" she cried out. "I knew there was something wrong. Harry has been acting strange since Christmas," she said. "Sam was here and mentioned the S.I.C. was working in the state."

Just at that moment they heard a gunshot. Benny ran to the library and found the judge at his desk with a bullet hole over his left ear.

"No need to call nine-eleven," Benny said. "He made sure he didn't have to stand trial. It is probably better this way for all concerned. Maybe we can keep some of it out of the papers for the sake of the kids; they are away at school," he told Tim.

Benny was still trying to save face for the governor. Tim knew that keeping it out of print was a pipe dream, but maybe Benny's saying he would try might get the governor's sister through the night easier.

Benny looked at the woman and said, "Get me the phone numbers of the children and I'll call and get them home right away."

Irma stood in the doorway of the judge's office and looked forty years older than when they first arrived.

"I'll stay here for the night, Irma," Benny said. He turned to Tim, "I'll be down town first thing in the morning for the arrangement at eight. Do you think you can handle the rest of the arrests without me tonight? I hate to leave the rest up to you, but I don't want to leave the governor's sister alone right now, for Sam's sake."

"Don't worry about a thing, Benny," Tim said. It was the first time he had used the attorney general's nickname, but right now he just seemed like a friend who was hurting for another friend. "I should be done and back at headquarters by five. If you have any questions you can reach me there. I'll feel better sticking close by until they are all apprehended. I'll leave two men outside."

Tim opened the door to leave the house, he saw the attorney general take the governor's sister up the long stairway to her room. He closed the door behind him and told two guards to stand outside and let no one in or out unless the attorney general gave them permission. He got back into his car, and was glad he had locked it on the way to the judge's. He wanted to be by himself for a while also. The remainder of the guardsmen followed behind him in their truck.

Leaving the estate they headed for the remainder of his stops. He made ten more arrests, of uniformed police officers and was back at the station by 4:45. They were quickly running out of cells.

Chapter Thirty-seven

The jail was really buzzing when Tim arrived with his prisoners, where he turned them over to waiting men he could trust. He walked over to three men standing by the water cooler.

"Read these three their rights and find them separate cells," he told two national guardsmen. Tim was surprised that the three detectives were still hanging around the office. They must have been pretty confident they had been missed in the round up; they weren't now.

The remaining few men wanted to know who was next and what was going to happen to their precinct. The news had traveled fast about the arrest of the D.A., chief, mayor, and the judge. Tim assured them he hoped they had made all the arrest necessary. He told them he was sure all the rotten apples were now in one barrel.

Thirty minutes later several officers came into the chief's office where Tim was lying on the sofa, trying to relax for a few minutes.

"We'd like to talk to you, sir, if you have a minute," one of the clean-cut looking uniformed officers said. "My name is Officer Brad Pullman, and we just wanted to thank you. Some of us have been thinking of quitting the force because of what we've seen going on around here. We just didn't know what else to do."

"I'm very glad you didn't. We're going to need a lot of help the next few months straightening out this disaster," Tim said.

"Whatever you need, sir. I know I speak for the rest of the guys. We'll be here to help in any way we can," young Brad said. "We may be able to fill in some of the blanks, too, if you need us."

Tim thanked them and said he would get together with them the next afternoon.

"The attorney general will want to talk to you, too," Tim said. "You men go home, get some rest, and be back in the morning. The guard and I can take over."

The men left and Tim lay back down for a quick nap.

Less than an hour later there was a noise in the hall. Waking quickly, Tim called out, "What's going on out there?"

Brad was standing there at the door with one of the national guardsmen. He had not gone home yet and had decided to stick around for the fun. Brad had the man in an arm-lock and was pushing him into the chief's office.

"I know this guy," he said. "He works for the mayor and does odd jobs for him. He was trying to get in to see him. He wanted to tell him what was happening."

What next? Tim thought. Those slime balls have infiltrated everywhere. "Good job," Tim praised Brad. "Bring him in. Let's see how much he wants to get off his chest."

Brad shoved the fellow, not too gently, into the room; pulled the blinds down on the door, and locked it. The national guardsman knew he was in big trouble. His name was Marve Bradberry. He wanted to make a deal.

"What you have for us will determine what kind of a deal you'll receive," Tim answered.

"How about a cop killing left to look like an accident?" Marve blurted out.

Tim's heart skipped a beat. Tim knew he was talking about Herb's murder. Tim would give him almost anything he asked for to get to the truth of his friend's death. Tim waited until his heart stopped racing and he could speak normally. Taking a deep breath, he asked calmly. "Depends on how much proof you have and what, where, and when the officer was killed."

Marve said sarcastically, "You know what, where, and when; he was your partner."

Bingo, thought Tim. "Okay, let's hear your story."

Marve described the scene where they had discovered the body of Herb. Tim was now sure this guy knew something. He said Sicky told them to give Herb knockout drops in his coffee after Sicky's boss told him how to lure Herb to his uncle's shop. Sicky did this by pretending to be one of Herb's informers and he told Herb he had something of importance to show him at the ship.

"How do you know all this?" Tim asked.

"Sicky and I did time together. When I got out he said he had some jobs for me and I wouldn't have to worry about being caught by the cops because he had all of them in this burg in his hip pocket. I went on a couple jobs with him and he was right. The cops were actually our lookouts."

"That still doesn't explain how you know Sicky killed my partner," Tim said.

Marve continued, "He had too much to drink at my house one night after a very profitable evening," Marve smiled. "He started bragging about how close he was to the big boss and he was the boss's right-hand man. He didn't know I had been tailing him for weeks. Sicky's one of those guys you never completely trust when your back is turned. Sicky said he told Herb his uncle would be gone all evening and they could stay there and talk about what was in it for Sicky if he turned on his uncle. Sicky's boss gave him the drops and told him how to use them; then waited in the back of the pawnshop till Herb was out cold. They put Herb in his own car and the boss drove him out in the country. Sicky followed in another car. They planned on the car going over the rail and catching fire, but it got stuck on the guardrail and they couldn't get it to go down the embankment. The cop's head had hit the wheel and they couldn't find a pulse so they left him and drove back to town in the boss's car. Sicky must have overdosed him for real by then; they both knew Herb was dead. The boss seemed really ticked."

Tim asked, "Did the mayor know about all this?"

"He was the one who sent Fred to Sam; and Sam called Sicky to tell him the boss wanted Herb put away," Marve answered.

That meant the mayor had a boss to whom he was obligated. Tim had to find out who that person was, and he told the man, "I'll do what I can for you. Tell Brad anything else you can think of that might help your case. I'll get a stenographer in here." Looking over at Brad he said, "Think you can handle all this?"

"You bet, sir," was the quick, sharp response. "I'll have everything for you by the time of the hearing."

"See if you can find out who the boss is," Tim said, in a whisper to Brad. "We need his name and where to find him."

Tim went into an adjoining office and called Benny. He told him of the latest development. "The rats are starting to fall like dominoes," Tim told the attorney general.

"We'll nail all those creeps now. I'll be right down," Benny said.

Tim knew Benny would not be sleeping either. "Did you get a hold of the judge's kids?" Tim asked.

"Yes, they will be here by the time their mother wakes up. I'm leaving a maid outside her door and the two guardsmen outside the house. I called the paper and told them of the unexpected death of the judge. It should be in the morning papers and I didn't want the family disturbed. The paper has promised to go easy on the story if I would give them an exclusive after the funeral. The governor will be up here by noon and I'll let him handle the papers. He was pretty shook up when I called, but he thinks what the judge did was probably for the best."

Chapter Thirty-eight

At nine in the morning, Sam, Fred, and J.P. swaggered into the courtroom; they took a seat and smiled at one another. The two had laughed most of the night and played cards in their cell. None of the three seemed to be worried.

"Judge Nancy Graff presiding," the bailiff announced. "All rise."

The three men seemed to have trouble getting to their feet. They no longer looked smug and confident. J.P.'s high-priced attorney asked if he could approach the bench. Judge Nancy knew what was coming and was looking forward to it.

"Approach," Judge Graff said.

"With do respect, Judge Graff, we would like to know why Judge Thompson is not presiding on this bench this morning," the lawyer said. "This is his courtroom!"

"Because he is dead!" Judge Graff stated calmly and loudly enough for all those in the courtroom to overhear. "Now, you may go back to your clients—Bailiff, read the charges."

The reading took very little time and the judge stood for no arguments from the defense table. Before any of the attorneys had a chance to say anything, she said, "Hearing in one week. Bail is set at two million for each defendant."

She would have liked to set bail higher, but that was the maximum allowed. Their attorney tried to argue, but she rapped her gavel, adjourned the session, and left. The three men were led out with a national guardsman on each side. One guard was heard to say, "They aren't going anywhere."

The attorney was still yelling at the bailiff, "I object and I want it on record."

"You'll have to take that up with the judge, and she's left the building for her other court. She has a full docket today and the rest of the week."

Chapter Thirty-nine

Marve, the bitter informant, had kept his eyes open more than anyone would have expected. He was one of the few who knew the real boss's name and where he hung out, along with the location of most of the loot. When Marve wasn't running errands for the chief or the D.A. he was tailing anyone he thought might help him get to the top rung of the crime ladder. It was not by chance he had spotted Sicky coming out of his uncle's shop that evening with another man. They were helping a man who looked drunk or unconscious into an old LTD. He pulled behind the second car as it pulled away from the shop, tailing the cars to the accident sight; and even got close enough to hear the Boss cuss out Sicky for using too much dope. He had watched the whole thing from a distance; the moon was so bright he had a clear picture of all the parties involved.

Later he carefully followed the car the boss drove while it returned to the shop and dropped off Sicky. He then tailed it to an estate in Wykoff. He left his car some distance from the gate; got in where the Boss had entered and began to snoop around. At the first barn he picked the lock to see what was in it. Again the moon was bright enough to see without a flashlight. No one noticed him prowling around the grounds and he was dog-tired when he returned to his car and slept around the clock when he got back to his apartment. He only had time to cover two of the barns and couldn't believe what he saw. It held treasurers beyond his imagination. He took some of the jewelry, figuring no one would miss it since there was so much there. He later confessed to Brad Pullman where the jewelry was stashed at his apartment. Brad sent an officer to pick up the evidence.

Tim was not able to hear all the judge had to say since he had taken two national guardsmen and was busy arresting the man called the Boss. Tim parked his car behind one of the barns up the road from the stables, and told the guardsman to watch his back; then headed for the horse stables. He had old clothes on and would pass as a gardener. First thing he did was to go into each of the horse stalls. Two men were mucking out: one told him that he thought Steve was in his apartment. Steve had been down earlier to tell them what needed done today and then went out toward his quarters. Tim thanked the man and approached the tall staircase. He quietly ascended.

Tim found Steve in his apartment over the stables. He was enjoying a snack of caviar and wine. His apartment was full of fine paintings and sculptures. Tim knew some of the pieces would be on the stolen properties list at headquarters. No wonder Steve didn't let anyone into his apartment. Steve played dumb as to why Tim should appear at his door showing a special investigator's badge.

"You got a lot of nerve busting into a man's home," Steve yelled.

"I have a warrant, Steve. I also have your gang behind bars."

"This is absurd. I have no gang."

"You should have been more careful, pal. You were followed the night you killed my partner," Tim told him.

"So that's it, a shakedown. How much do you want to keep your mouth shut?" Steve said. It was one of the few times Tim wanted to hit a suspect.

"You don't have enough money," Tim told him. "I can't be bought like you did the D.A., chief, and judge."

Steve heard the names and made a dash for his desk. Tim knew it was to get a gun.

"Go ahead, Steve. I'd like nothing better than to save the taxpayers money on a trial," he said, while pulling out his service revolver from the back of his belt, aiming it at Steve. "Now come over here and lean against this wall."

Steve walked over to where Tim stood holding the gun. Taking the cuffs from his back pocket, Tim put them on Steve's wrists which he pulled behind Steve's back; all the time reading him his rights. "Do you understand all your rights?" Tim asked.

"Yeah!" Steve growled. "Let's get this over with, so I can get back here before my wine gets too warm."

Tim smiled and put the cork back in the bottle. "I'll put this in the refrigerator. It will be far too warm by the time you will be able to drink any of it again."

He took Steve down the stairs and past the stables to his parked car. The men looked out from one of the stalls and saw Steve being led away in handcuffs. Steve shouted at them to get back to work. Both men lowered their heads and started raking. They hoped he would never return.

Chapter Forty

The trial lasted all of three weeks. All the men were found guilty. There were so many charges against each one it was hard to sort them out. Tim and the S.I.C. went for the maximum over Herb's death and got it. It would be many years before some of them would ever see the light of day as free men. The higher-ups would probably not last long in prison anyway since they would be in with men whom they had put in jail while they themselves were bigger crooks. The police officers were also headed for a bad time and each received fifteen years. Sicky and Steven both received life for the murder of Herb. With Steve receiving back to back life sentences because it seems Steve had also helped Elizabeth's husband Jasper die a little before his time. When Steve saw all the treasurers to be had on the estate and what a great place the old man's estate would be to hide all his loot from other robberies, he planned the owner's death and was not upset when Elizabeth was killed. It made it easier for him. She had begun to be concerned after all the complaints from the stablemen and gardeners. He knew she was thinking of getting rid of him and it did not surprise him when she excluded him from her will.

He ran the whole gang from his little domain over the stables on the back of the estate. When checking the barns they found them loaded with stolen merchandise. It would take months to inventory and return all the items to their rightful owners. The S.I.C. had gotten to them just in time. They found shipping schedules in Steve's apartment. The first shipment was to have been transferred that week.

Chapter Forty-one

Cindy and Rene returned home the day the trial was over. Rene was now a permanent resident and settled in as manager. She got right to work hiring a new staff and, by the end of the month, the old staff was finally able to retire to Florida. Cindy was busy redoing the west wing of the old mansion for their personal rooms. She at last was at peace with the way Herb died and looking forward to the future as the head of her little empire. Tim was still at police headquarters and, for some reason, had decided to stay in Crescent. He came over for Nora's cooking not less than once a week; at least that's why he said he came.

It was Wednesday, the twenty-seventh of July, and Cindy had not mentioned Rene's birthday.

After breakfast, she suggested they put on slacks and boots to tramp over the property.

"I have to check on the stables and two of our farms. Come on and go with me. We'll make a day of it and stop at the Cozy Café for lunch."

"Do I have to wear boots?" Rene asked.

"If you want to save your good shoes, you do. I don't know what we will be getting into," she told her.

"Okay, give me twenty minutes and I'll be ready."

"I'll met you in the parlor," Cindy said.

Twenty minutes later Rene arrived in jeans, shirt, and boots.

"You look great," Cindy told her.

"Yeah, sure!" Rene mumbled and followed Cindy out the side door.

When Cindy walked outside she stood to one side and let Rene go out into the bright sunlight first. A loud chorus of "Happy Birthday" permeated the air.

The staff were standing outside waiting for Rene. When they parted Rene saw a beautiful Harley Lowrider in cherry red, sitting on its standard.

"My name's on this thing," Rene said.

"Yes! I got us both one. I was afraid mine wouldn't arrive in time for us to ride on your birthday," she smiled at her friend, "but it did."

Cindy had to purchase a full-sized Harley because of her height. She knew Rene had to sell their bikes after Fred died, and she had always regretted it.

"Cindy, you stinker! Thank you," was all Rene could say. Tears appeared in her eyes as she hugged her friend.

"Here is your leather. I cleaned it for you," Nora said, helping her into the jacket.

"Thank you, Nora," Rene said. "You did a beautiful job."

"Here's a new helmet from the staff," Jan said. "We got you a white one to match your leather."

"Thank you all," Rene said. "I don't know what to say."

"They were all in on this," Cindy told her.

"How did you ever keep it a secret?" Rene said turning to Cindy.

"It wasn't easy. You seemed to be everywhere this past week. Come on, let's go for a ride," Cindy laughed.

The two women mounted their bikes, secured their helmets and started their engines. Kicking the bikes off the standards they rode out toward the airstrip to the applause of the staff.

As they approached the airstrip a little lady walked out from the hanger.

"Mom," Rene cried. "How did you get here?" she said as she circled her on her bike.

The two women stopped and got off their bikes, running over to hug Rene's mother.

"Cindy, this is too much," Rene said.

Randy walked out of the hanger.

"She loved the flight," he said. "She wanted to learn to fly the plane." They all laughed. "I'll get the car and take your mom up to the house," he told Rene.

"Oh no, you won't. I'll just hop on the back of Norene's bike and she can take me there. This looks like even more fun than riding in a plane," she told them and climbed onto the back of Rene's bike.

Cindy lead the way as the three women headed for the manor.

Gloria came out and stood next to Randy and they both shook their heads and she said, "Well, now we know where Rene and Cindy get their adventuresome spirit." They laughed and went over to their car to go up and join Rene's party.

THE END